Anna

A Doctor's Quest into the Unknown

Michael Derechin

ANNA
A DOCTOR'S QUEST INTO THE UNKNOWN

iUniverse books may be ordered through booksellers or by contacting:

iUniverse LLC
1663 Liberty Drive
Bloomington, IN 47403
www.iuniverse.com
1-800-Authors (1-800-288-4677)

Because of the dynamic nature of the Internet, any web addresses or links contained in this book may have changed since publication and may no longer be valid. The views expressed in this work are solely those of the author and do not necessarily reflect the views of the publisher, and the publisher hereby disclaims any responsibility for them.

Cover Photography © 2014 Michael Derechin. Graphic Engineering by Ioana Voicu.

ISBN: 978-1-4917-2788-1 (sc)
ISBN: 978-1-4917-2790-4 (hc)
ISBN: 978-1-4917-2789-8 (e)

Library of Congress Control Number: 2014904546

Printed in the United States of America.

iUniverse rev. date: 06/12/2014

Contents

Acknowledgments

This book never would have been completed without my patients and their families. They were the bold and the brave. I learned from them, and they gave back generously.

I am grateful to have the continued support of my wife, Nessa, whose faith and ideas helped the story's development, improved the flow of suspense, and calmed my hysteria.

Thanks also to the members of Writing Group II on Sanibel Island, who shared helpful constructive criticism, and my friends who told me to shut up and put pen to paper.

Chapter 1

"I brought this curse on myself. God is punishing me!"

Willie Mays "Bernie" Bernstein, MD, fell back into his chair. He looked at his patient, Marge Whitestone, and then at her husband sitting next to her. His mouth opened and shut. Bernie thought, *Shit, not again. No, Marge, you didn't do it. God doesn't care about you. In fact, he or she doesn't know you exist. God is screwing you, along with everyone else. Don't take it personally. You see, Marge, there is no God, so get over it.*

The thought lingered until he found his voice. "Marge, cancer is not your doing. It has nothing to do with sin... Is there something you'd like to talk about?"

She shook her head. Bernie shrugged, looked again at his patient, and then stared at the floor. *She looks awful. Last month, full of energy—now a shadow of what was. The good old Hippocratic oath: "First, do no harm..." Hippocrates never heard of cancer docs—we hurt, then they die.*

He looked at the old woman, at the same time gripping his oak desk. Her hair was now gray, her eyes red and sinking into their sockets, her skin turning gray to yellow.

I failed again. It's 1973, and Nixon speaks about a cure for cancer in the next decade. What bullshit.

1

Bernie felt cold. He started to shake and knew fear was in him. George Whitestone looked at the doctor. "You're pale. Are you all right?"

Bernie nodded. "Marge, the tests came back. The cancer is growing." His gaze returned to the desk.

"I know, doc. The pains are back, and I got no appetite. I'm just one of my old horses ready to be hauled away. What's next?"

Bernstein took a deep breath. "Make you as comfortable as possible. I've exhausted all drugs used in cancer of the cervix. As I told you before, you could get another opinion at the university."

Marge and George shook their heads no.

Tears ran down George's face as he held his wife's arm tightly. His right eye twitched; his tanned faced aged in seconds.

"Doc, Marge was lookin' so good a month ago. She looked a lot worse when you first saw her. You helped her good. You got to do something." He spoke the words through sobs and tears.

Damn you, George. Stop your sniveling. Shit, don't tell me how she looked. I thought she'd be cured. I should have known better.

He calmed down and was able to control his voice. "I've looked at different research drugs. There aren't any that have promise in cancer of the cervix."

His mind wandered back to the way he introduced himself to patients during his first few months in practice. He told them that he was an oncologist and treated cancer. Many of the doctors grew upset with this approach, telling Bernstein that he'd never get a another consult. "After all, you don't tell patients they have cancer, especially when I just told them they had a bad infection."

Bernstein's response was always the same: "I'm not about to tell patients that they have an infection and then give them drugs that'll make their hair fall out, get them deathly sick, and continue insisting that it's a bad cold."

The doctors weren't the only ones that lied; families insisted on it. "If you tell Ma she has cancer, she'll die."

Marge Whitestone was different. Her voice jarred him away from his reverie. "How long do I have?"

Shaking his head, he replied, "I don't know. The average is six or eight months. No one is the average—might be a lot longer."

Marge looked at him. "You didn't answer me earlier. My sins have come back to me. Why else would I be punished so much?"

"Marge, there isn't a known cause for cancer of the cervix or, for that matter, any cancer. It might be associated with a virus, but it's certainly not the result of sin. Is there something you'd like to talk to me about in private?"

Bernie looked at George, hoping he'd understand and leave, but it was not to be. Marge shook her head again.

"Maybe another day."

She needed more pain medication. Bernstein wrote the prescription for much more than she needed. Warning that too much could be fatal, he wrote for three refills.

Marge looked at the piece of paper and nodded. Bernie realized that he had made his point.

By this time Bernstein's back was painful, his shirt soaked. He sat back in his overstuffed chair, trying to relax.

It never gets easier. Why am I trying to treat cancer?

He looked at the diplomas hanging on the pale yellow walls of his office: college, medical school, internship, residency, and a postdoctoral degree, all from the best programs. *Not much good when treating cancer.*

The intercom buzzed him back to the present. He pushed the buttons of the machine, gave up, and ran into the hall, yelling at his secretary, "Maria, is it an emergency?"

"Doctor, it's Leah, your wife."

"Maria, I'm fully aware of my wife's name. Tell her *later*. I'll call later," he said and went back into the room. "I've asked Maria not to interrupt a hundred times. It doesn't sink in. I'm sorry."

"She means well, doc. When do you want to see me again?"

He started to give her a date, then stopped, looked at her again, and tore up the appointment. "Don't push yourself, Marge. I'll stop by the house within the next two weeks—earlier, if needed."

George looked at him as they both headed for the door. "Our daughter Jo wanted to be here, but the kids stayed home from school today; they're sick. Can she call later?"

"Of course, George. Have her call about six this evening."

Marge gave him a hug. He held back. The couple left the room.

She's going to die. I can't stand it. Another death. I feel damn helpless.

Before calling home, he took a few deep breaths and then dialed the number. Leah answered on the first ring; the dogs had diarrhea but not the cats or the raccoon.

"It's the food," said Leah. "All my beautiful German shepherds are sick."

"So change the food. Why call me like it's an emergency?"

"Well, no need to get so huffy. I won't call you again." The call ended with a bang.

"I'm acting like an asshole," he mumbled.

Lunchtime. The waiting room was empty. Bernstein punched the intercom, which responded with a squawk.

"Screw this goddamned contraption," he said and then yelled through the closed door, "Maria, break time. No interruptions for twenty minutes, unless emergencies."

She walked into his office. "Doctor, you don't have to scream. The intercom works fine."

"I don't trust these things. Besides, it doesn't work for me." He was still holding the intercom receiver and screaming.

"Dr. Bernstein, stop screaming into the intercom. I'm standing in front of you."

"Oh right, sorry." He took his hand off the button. "Maria, please, no calls. I need the break. Only emergencies—and there are very few cancer emergencies."

His secretary nodded and left the room, slamming the door shut.

Bernstein stripped to his briefs, sat on the floor crossed-legged, and started to meditate, counting his breaths, feeling his abdomen expand and relax, continuing to count his breaths.

Relax... relax... in... out... in... out...

Marge, damn it, dying soon, can't do a thing...

One... two...

Two of them. Christ, she looked good for a year and more. I thought cure—stupid.

Deep breath... in... out...

His back pain lessened.

Slow breathing—count the ins, let out the bad air, bring in the clean.

The intercom screeched.

Bernstein jolted upright, ran to the door, and pulled it open.

"Now what?"

"Doctor, put your pants on."

He stood there, refusing to move. "What is the problem?"

Maria rolled her eyes, gave a sigh. "It's Jessica Coles on line two. She's the head nurse..."

"I know she's the head nurse. Is this an emergency?"

"Jessica wants to speak to you about a consult. She said it was important."

He wondered what the penalty would be for strangling his secretary; decided that, under the circumstances, it would be a small fine; slammed the door; and picked up the phone.

"What's up, Jessica?"

"Dr. Mortimer wants you to see a patient. Please, Bernie, see her tonight."

Very few nurses called him Bernie, but Jessica was one. She had taken him under her wing when he was first starting out, put up with his hysterics, and treated him as the son she never had.

The nurse went on. "Her name is Anna Bing, and she's eleven."

Bernstein stood, shaking his head no as though they were face to face.

"Jessica, no children. You know I don't treat kids."

"It's my granddaughter."

He stopped shaking his head and sat on the side of his desk. Jessica brought him up to date.

Apparently, the girl had developed large masses in her neck, started losing weight and, when she saw the family doctor, was diagnosed as having an infection. She was given antibiotics, which didn't work. The swellings enlarged, and her mother brought her to Dr. Mortimer. He promptly admitted the child to the hospital and sent a consult to Bernstein.

Jessica started crying. "Bernie, please see her. Let us know what you think. She's all we have."

He started shaking his head again. Without saying anything, he stood up and paced about the room, the phone still held to his ear and the overly long extension cord following close behind.

Bernstein stopped, looked at an old photo that stood atop his desk. It showed a small group of kids, about eight or nine, smiling. Among them were Bernstein and Zack.

"Shit!"

His mind focused on that time.

"Mama, what's wrong with Zack? He lost all his hair, and he's walking funny."

His mother spit twice, always a bad sign. "You shouldn't know. Go play. Forget about him. You're only eight."

"But he's my best friend." Bernie had visited him every day—until Zack died.

He kept the picture of his friend on his desk.

Bernstein went back to pacing, still shaking his head, and tried to tell Jessica that he didn't have enough experience treating children with cancer.

He remembered a friend cornering him in medical school. "Hey, Bernie, guess who's stuck with the pediatric oncology floor— Willie Mays Bernstein, junior medical student!"

He never forgot the six weeks with the cancer kids. Bernstein bit his lip and picked up a Spalding ball cradled in a holder on his desk. It was the hollow, all-purpose pink ball of his youth, and he threw it against the wall. *Fuck it.*

He told Jessica he'd see Anna that evening in the hospital. Bernie hung up the phone and felt a cold hand on his shoulder. He looked back into darkness—nothing.

When the office hours ended, Bernstein made his way across the parking lot thinking of Anna and the futility of oncology. He stopped. "Something's wrong," he muttered. "It's the trees... the branches lost their hair."

A cold wind blew through his coat, and he couldn't stop shaking. "Shit, it's only November." Winter was coming early, and the barren landscape of New England drew him further into darkness. The knot in his chest tightened. It was fear—fear of hurting, of killing, of failure.

"I can't treat a kid. Let someone else do it." He spoke the words into the wind. No one heard. Only the wind knew it was not to be.

Driving to the hospital, one mile away, Bernstein told himself that he'd keep his distance. No emotion. Say hello to the family, look at the x-rays and the medical chart, examine the kid, tell them he couldn't help, and send her to Bayside University Hospital. *Great plan, Bernie.*

Feeling better, he thought it best to call his wife and apologize, which he did on arriving at the hospital. "Leah, I'm sorry I was short. Bad day."

She let his voice sit out on the airwaves before answering. "I'm getting used to your lousy disposition. By the way, Russell showed up this afternoon."

Bernstein shook his head. "Is he okay?"

Leah seemed to lighten up. "The usual. He had a fight with Rob. Russell caught him with another man and is hysterical. Besides that, he's showing a few dogs at the greater Boston show this weekend. He's not going to be in a rush to leave."

Russell was a dog handler, one of the best in the business. Leah was his best friend.

"So what's new? This happens every two months. He'll get over it. Rob will drive up to the house, there'll be a big scene, and they'll go home. Meanwhile, we'll have gourmet meals."

"He's already planned the menu for the week. I sent him to pick up the boys from school. They missed the bus."

"Now I know everything is back to normal. Did David have problems with the late note I wrote today?"

"You didn't write the note, and the two of you have to stop. David was given detention because of your shenanigans. He wrote the note, and you signed it."

"So what's wrong with that?"

"You signed it 'David's father.' They gave him detention."

"Those teachers have no sense of humor."

The call ended. He'd be late for dinner.

The hospital loudspeaker notified him that he had an outside call. It was Jo Adams, Marge Whitestone's daughter. He answered immediately.

"Dr. Bernstein, I spoke to my father a few hours ago. He's beside himself. I'm just as worried about him as I am my mother."

Bernie sat down in an overstuffed chair in the lounge. He fished the Spalding out of his pocket and started tossing it.

"I know, Jo. He was broken up when they were in the office. Marge accepted the prognosis better than he did. They're both going to need help."

"Mother said there's not much you can do other than make her comfortable. I've accepted it and wasn't surprised. It's still hard to take."

"I know. I can't accept it either. I want to ask you something. Marge seems to believe she's sinned and that brought on the cancer. Are you aware of a reason she'd think that?"

"No. I do know that since she was diagnosed, she's referred to sin. In fact, she now goes to church regularly. My mother was never a churchgoer."

Bernie nodded and looked at his watch. He had spent too much time, and there was work to be done. "Okay, Jo. Let me know if I can help. Otherwise I'll be there in two weeks." He hung up the phone.

Bernstein couldn't delay any longer. He had to see Anna and decided to start in the x-ray department looking at her chest films. They showed a mass in the middle of her chest.

Shit.

From there he went to the nurses' station and grabbed Anna's chart. She had been feverish for three weeks, had not responded to a big-time antibiotic, had lost five pounds over the same time period, and was now anemic.

Fever, weight loss, anemia. All bad signs.

"This sucks," he said to no one in particular. Pam Nichols, the charge nurse, ignored him.

Finally, Bernie took a deep breath and headed toward the kid's room. Pam Nichols followed him. The walls of the corridor were hospital dismal: cold and gray. The lightbulbs cast a pale yellow glow throughout the hall, flickering off and on at times. Some were out. It was chilly inside those walls, and he again buttoned up.

Keep going, Bernstein. Just see the kid and go home.

Jessica and another woman stopped him.

"Bernie, this is my daughter, Bella, Anna's mother." Bella was a large woman, a good six feet tall with broad, muscular shoulders and large hands. Her face was ruddy and her eyes bloodshot. She smelled of wine.

Bella jabbed the doctor in the chest with her hand, catching him off guard and driving him against the wall. Instinctively, he pushed her away.

"I don't want any bullshit with my daughter. Take a look at her, and then get her out of this shitty hospital to Bayside University Medical Center. I don't want any of you hacks."

"Bella, stop it! He'll do what's best." Jessica stood between her daughter and the doctor. "I'm sorry, Bernie, we've been on edge ever since Anna became ill. She's our life."

"I understand," he lied. "I'll see Anna and be back to speak to you." He continued toward her room.

I really need this crap. Bella, you just made my life a lot easier. I can send Anna to the university without a second thought.

He resolved to be cold, aloof.

Sorry, kid. We can't help you here; got to send you to Bayside. They'll make you better.

His back stiffened, and he marched to the room with the women following him.

Bernie suddenly turned. "Please wait outside. Let me see Anna with Pam." He pointed to the nurse tagging behind.

Jessica and Bella backed off.

I can't believe it. They listened.

Anna was sitting up in bed. She had thick brown hair and dark eyes to match. Her face was pure sunshine, especially her mouth. She was clutching a teddy bear.

"Hi, Dr. Bernie." She hesitated, looked him over, and went on. "You don't look like a doctor. Are you sure?" she said with a twinkle.

"Damn, I've been putting it over on everyone. Now a smart-ass kid catches me."

"Well, it's easy. No tie, wearing jeans, and a beard. A beard! Doctors don't have beards. Nope, you can't be a doctor." She tried to hold in a laugh.

"How about Jerry Garcia?"

"He's a musician. The lead in the *Grateful Dead*."

"You're kidding. I thought he was a doctor. He's always talking about drugs."

Anna couldn't control her laugh.

The nurse, meanwhile, had taken a standing position on the far side of the bed.

Anna continued the patter. "What about the clothes? I wanna see your diploma."

"I loved the sixties and couldn't part with the clothes. Did graduate. Class of '63. Correspondence course. No diploma but a very nice letter. I'll show it to you tomorrow."

"That was ten years ago. When did you get the letter?"

"Yesterday—don't open my mail much."

She threw the bear at him.

Bella popped her head into the room. She'd been standing outside. "Cut the crap, Bernstein. Just examine her."

Anna answered quickly, "Mom, go away, we're just having fun."

Bella disappeared, and Anna motioned him to come closer.

"I've got to raise both of them."

"Looks like a full-time job."

The young girl nodded.

Bernstein's aloofness was long gone. He examined her. She had large, firm, rubbery masses in her neck, abdomen, and groin.

Anna has cancer.

He asked Bella and Jessica to come into the room. Bella wanted to speak in the hall, away from her daughter. Bernstein would have none of it, and the mother reluctantly came in, sat on the bed, and stroked Anna's hair.

He explained to the three that it was best to take a biopsy of one of the lymph nodes in her neck. That was the only way to make a diagnosis. It was a simple procedure and could be performed the next day.

"It will likely turn out to be either Hodgkin's disease or a lymphoma, both of which are usually very treatable. Bob Mortimer could do the surgery."

"Oh no, that's not going to happen. She's going to Bayside. I don't want either of you, and I'd like to speak to you in the hall." With that, Bella turned and stomped out of the room. Bernstein slowly followed. Pam and Jessica stayed in the room with Anna.

In the hall, her eyes full of fire, Bella started up. She pointed an accusing finger at Bernstein. "Look, you. I don't want any cozy crap with my daughter. She's getting out of here."

Bernstein took a deep breath, pushed her finger away. "I'm getting tired of your histrionics. If you want to take her out of here, then do so, but it's not a good idea."

Bella turned away from his glare and then moved a few feet toward the room. Bernstein put his hand on her shoulder, turning her around.

"I'm not finished. We don't even know the diagnosis. I'm sure it's one of the two I mentioned, but teaching hospitals like to know what they're getting."

Bella started to go back to the room.

Bernie had more to say. "Bella, most patients are better off at the community hospital, if possible. We do know how to take care of Anna's problem, and she'll have both you and Jessica around." With that, he went into the room. Bella followed.

Anna was waiting for them. "Mom, calm down. I could hear you two arguing. Don't forget, I'm the sick one. He makes me feel good, and so far, he's the only one that knows what's happening."

Bella's mouth opened. Jessica nodded her approval. Bella's mouth shut with a bang.

Arrangements were made for the biopsy to be performed in the morning. Bernie then headed home.

Snow started falling.

I need a drink.

He pulled into a liquor store, bought a nip and a beer, went back to the car, took a big swallow, and headed into what was now a storm.

Why am I doing this? Let her go. That's not possible. I know I'm right. She's much better here than Bayside.

He started to relax and took another sip of beer.

On the drive home, he thought of Marge Whitestone and the first time he met her. The consult came while he was looking over another patient's chart. A nurse suddenly appeared in front of him, hands on her hips. She was Katherine Boor, nurse to Dr. Hampton, the chief of medicine. Due to her position, Boor felt entitled to be second-in-command.

"Dr. Bernstein, you're to see a patient in room 312. She's in a private room."

He saluted. "Yes, sir—312, private room." He scratched his forehead. "How do I recognize No Name, room 312?"

"Stop treating me like this. I demand respect. Her name is Whitestone; she'll be the one in the bed."

Bernstein dropped the salute. "Gotcha, Captain. Any orders?"

"Dr. Hampton wants you to see her but not tell her she has that disease. There's nothing you can do anyway."

"Whitestone—is that her first or last name?"

"Stop playing with me. Her name is Mrs. Marge Whitestone."

"Oh, and what disease might she have?"

"Don't play dumb; she has the big C."

"My gosh, she has the clap?"

Boor informed him that he was disgusting. "Bernstein, if you mention anything about cancer, we'll never send you another consult."

"If those are the conditions, I won't see her. Tell Hampton to do his own dirty work—or better yet, put him on the phone and I'll tell him."

"He's much too busy to speak to people like you. Just remember, if you don't see her, that'll be the last referral you'll ever get from him. If I had my way, you'd be long gone by now."

"Madame Defarge, are you knitting my name?"

"I don't know what you're talking about. You're crazy. Are you going to see her or not?"

"Yes, on my terms."

He saw her later that day. "Hi, I'm Dr. Bernstein. Dr. Hampton asked me to see you."

She gave him a long look. "Sonny, sit here." She pointed to the side of the bed. "That old bastard didn't want me to see you. I was the one that demanded the consult. You the cancer doc?"

"Er... er, yes."

"Well, I have cancer. Can you help me?"

And he did, for more than two years.

The scene faded from his mind.

The storm had grown stronger by the time he arrived at his home. It was a large, wood-sided house set on a hill with the driveway running into a breezeway. A rock wall that he had built with his sons held back the hillside. Bushes of laurel and rhododendron drooped over the walls.

As he opened the door of his car, the wind caught it and literally pulled him out. He climbed the wooden stairs to the first floor. The lights were all on, and a fire crackled in the fireplace. Three-month-old puppy Orion spotted Bernie and attacked, trying to lick him to death.

The boys were busy but looked up when he approached. Allan and Jack were playing football in the family room.

No blood or holes on the wall. Good signs.

"Hi, Dad. Good day?"

"Yep, how about you two?"

In unison, they said, "Great."

Next he found eight-year-old David cutting a pair of new pants at the knees.

"Hi, watcha doin'?"

"Cuttin'."

"How come?"

"Don't like 'em."

"Oh."

Ten-year-old Mark was in the family room resting on the overstuffed cushioned couch, reading a book entitled *Dinosaurs of the Early Reptilian Age*. His head rested on Champion Quinella of Brazenhaus's chest. The German shepherd was busy watching Walter Cronkite on the six-thirty CBS evening news. Bernie gave them both a kiss and received a lick from the dog and a smile from Mark.

"Did Quinella turn on the news?"

"Funny, Dad. She wouldn't let me read until I turned it on. You know how much she loves Cronkite."

Bernie smiled. "So does everyone else. Why should Quinella be different?"

From there, he headed into the kitchen. Russell was in his jockey shorts and T-shirt putting the finishing touches on supper. Leah was setting the table. Two dogs, Sam and Jolly, were stretched out in the kitchen, blocking all traffic.

Sounds from the living room made him turn to find Expert, their other German shepherd, snoring on the couch; the three cats were curled up next to him. The house raccoon, Margrate, sat in an open dog crate nearby munching peanut brittle.

The dogs were champions. The cats and raccoon were not. Bernie had found the baby raccoon on the roadside trying to nurse from its dead mother. He had brought the baby home against Leah's protest; the overgrown rat was there to stay. The cats came from everywhere.

Russell spotted Bernstein.

"Bernie, darling. You've arrived. Oh, my poor doctor looks so tired." He ran over to give Bernstein a hug and then stopped. "Bernie, you've been drinking. Leah, we can't have this—our doctor has been drinking and driving in a snowstorm. I won't allow it." Bernstein gave him a hug.

"Russell, stop it. I had one nip on the way home. Don't make such a fuss."

Leah shook her head, a look of disgust on her face. "He's been doing this nip on the way home more often lately. I can't wait till he gets home." She looked away and then back at him. "We'll talk about this later," she said and gave him a kiss. "I do love you," she whispered.

He held her tightly and tried to tell her how much he needed her. Words failed. Tears fell down his cheeks. He thought of an eleven-year-old lying in a hospital bed with cancer and gripped Leah tighter. "Please, don't leave me."

"Never, but I'm so afraid you'll get into an accident."

He promised, as always, he'd be careful.

The rest of the night was relatively normal other than supper. It was a Russell special: cucumber, tomatoes, and sliced sweet onions sprinkled with a good dose of oregano, garlic, a pinch of black pepper, fresh lemon juice, and a few drops of virgin olive oil. Creamy imported feta cheese in small cubes blanketed the top.

The salad was followed by filet of wild salmon topped with drawn-down molasses and orange slices. Cut yellow gold potatoes and asparagus made to perfection rounded out the meal. Leah prevented the chef from making dessert other than fresh fruit.

Russell had put on a pair of pants and shirt for the supper. "Bernie, you better eat the salmon. I spent a good part of the day looking for the right pieces."

Bernstein rubbed his forehead. "Okay, okay, I give up. You know I don't eat meat, but you make it anyway. I will this time, but try—just try—to behave."

Russell smiled. "Fish is not a meat. It's a fish, so stop sulking and eat it."

"Yes, dear," said Bernie, and he threw Russell a kiss.

During the meal, they spoke about the Vietnam War. Allan, who was fourteen, didn't understand why the United States was in the war. "I heard Dad telling one of his friends that it was crazy."

Jack, age thirteen, joined in. "My teacher said that the Communists would take over if we didn't stop them."

David looked at his father. "Dad, you were in the army. How did you feel?"

Bernie shook his head. "I don't want to speak about the war, but I don't feel your teacher should be talking about it unless as a history lesson."

After dinner, Russell and Leah cleaned up, the boys did their homework, and Bernie supervised. Afterward he read them a story out of Kipling's *The Jungle Book.* Then the boys went to bed.

An hour later, the others followed. Russell had a reserved room overlooking the family room complete with a fireman's pole.

Bernstein lay awake thinking about the next day's schedule. *I'll get up early, go to the Y, exercise, then head to my office.*

Thoughts of Anna kept creeping into his head.

"What a fuckin' day," he mumbled. Eventually he turned, held onto Leah, and was soon asleep.

Chapter 2

The slides of the lymph nodes were ready for review two days later. Toni Carter was the pathologist. Bernstein felt she was one of the best he'd come across and could never understand why she chose to work in a small hospital. But she did, and he was delighted. On this day, he went straight to her office.

"Bernstein, you're a pain in the ass. Stop hanging over me. You're like those school boys I had to deal with."

He smiled. "Toni, I can't blame the boys for drooling over you. Blond braids, blue eyes, and a gorgeous face—the perfect *shikseh*. Now get the fuck out of my way."

"What's a *shikseh?*"

"The kind of beauty that would make my mother threaten to put her head in the oven if I brought home." He gave her a playful shove.

She moved over but not far enough. He still felt her body next to his but didn't complain.

He purred. She smiled.

It took time to differentiate between a lymphoma and Hodgkin's disease. The best indicators were Reed-Sternberg cells, mainly seen in Hodgkin's disease.

He grabbed more of Anna's slides and another microscope, muttering about her perfume, and sat a short distance away.

More time passed and Bernstein announced, "Hodgkin's disease—I'm sure of it."

"Bernie, it's not typical. I don't see cells that I'd call Reed-Sternberg."

"Yeah, but there's enough of those large, irregular cells that are not the typical cells of Hodgkin's but are close. Jeez, Toni, I just feel it is Hodgkin's. I certainly wouldn't call it one way or the other without both of us agreeing." He stopped, took a deep breath, and looked again at the slide, moving it about under the lens. "Take a look here. These few look like Reed-Sternberg cells."

She came over, looked through the microscope, and nodded. "Okay, not quite but almost. Leave me alone; I'll call you once I've had a chance to spend more time with them. Bernie, without typical Reed-Sternberg cells, I'm uncomfortable making the diagnosis. I still don't understand why you're so convinced."

"I'll tell you why. I've dealt with lymphoma and Hodgkin's throughout my training, plus the years I've been in practice. There are other findings besides Reed-Sternberg cells. If you look closely, you'll see large, irregular-looking cells along with a number of white blood cells that aren't seen in lymphomas but are in Hodgkin's."

He took a sip of her coffee and promptly spit it in the sink. "This coffee is terrible, and it's cold."

"Okay, big shot, buy lunch for both of us, and I'll make hot coffee."

Bernstein smiled. "You got a deal and a date for tomorrow." He got back to the point. "Toni, I can't explain all the reasons. I'm sure it's Hodgkin's. Maybe it's intuition, but I feel I'm right."

She looked at him again. "Why is it so important? Both diseases are similar. Can't they be treated the same?"

"No. There are differences in the chemotherapy and in the results. Hodgkin's can be cured, while a lymphoma cannot."

Toni gave him a puzzled look.

"Hodgkin's often involves exploratory surgery to measure the extent of the disease but can be cured with aggressive chemotherapy. Lymphoma, on the other hand, can be controlled with therapy and much less surgery but not likely cured."

He stopped and took another drink of her coffee. "Jeez, this stuff is awful. Toni, don't forget we're dealing with an eleven-year-old. She has her whole life ahead of her."

"Bernie, from what I hear and see, you put a lot of effort into your patients, but you seem to be more attached to this case. What's it about?"

"She reminds me of someone." He stopped and just shrugged. His mind went back to Zack and the cancer kids. "I can't tell you all the whys, but I feel that I can take care of her." He shook his head. "Damn it! I feel so right about this kid."

"Bernie, you're getting too wound up. You've got to take a step back or you'll break."

He shrugged. "Yes, dear."

Toni smiled, told him to go to hell. "If you hang around any longer, I won't get any work done, so get your ass out of here."

With that, he gave her a kiss on the forehead and was gone.

Two hours later, Toni called to say she agreed that Anna had Hodgkin's. Bernstein gave a thumbs-up to no one and smiled as he reminded her about lunch the next day.

Chapter 3

Early the next morning, Bernie went for a five-mile run, showered, dressed, and drove to the hospital.

He went straight to Anna's room. There were windows on the north and west side. It seemed to catch the evening gloom and miss the morning sun. The head of her bed was against the far wall, away from the light and the radiators. A pale green blanket covered her.

Without saying a word, he sat on the bed next to her. Jessica and Bella were camped alongside. They looked right at him. His eyes were glassy; black rings circled the bags beneath his lids. His stethoscope hung from his drooped shoulders.

"Anna, you have a form of cancer. It's called Hodgkin's disease." Bella turned her head quickly, jumped from the bed, grabbed Bernstein's arm, and pulled him out the door and into the hall. Once outside, she screamed, still clutching his arm. "What is wrong with you? You did the same thing yesterday. You're an ass. 'Anna, you have cancer,'" she said, mimicking Bernstein. She caught her breath. "You're insane if you think I'd let you care for my daughter." Bernstein pulled his arm away.

Bella started crying softly, becoming louder, more uncontrolled. Bernstein could feel the heat in his face. He bit his lip, took deep breaths, and then slowly put his arms on her shoulders. He took them off immediately.

"Bella, we went through this yesterday. You never allow me to finish speaking. I think she'll be okay, but I can't lie about the diagnosis. Fortunately, it's Hodgkin's, not an aggressive lymphoma."

"Bernstein, I love Anna. She's all I have. This isn't right. I won't let her die." The crying became sobs, and Bella tried to control herself. Her eyes were red, and she glared at him. "Who the hell do you think you are that you know so much?" Again, she attempted to mimic him. "She'll be fine." She stopped, and her face turned crimson. "Screw you. You're nothing but a shit in a pissant hospital. Why should I give you a chance?"

He'd had enough. "You don't see the picture at all. You're giving me a chance? It's Anna who needs the chance. I know what I'm doing, as do many doctors at Bayside. I can keep her at this hospital and have your family around at all times." He stopped and thought of Bella making rounds with him, complaining all the while. He cringed. He wiped the sweat off his face. Bella's mouth became tight, and she glared into his eyes. Bernie went on. "Last night I spoke to Bob Mortimer about the diagnosis. He's performed many exploratory operations for Hodgkin's and feels that he has assembled a first-rate team here."

He took more deep breaths. *Shit, I can't catch my breath. She's driving me nuts.*

He stopped, chewed on his tongue. It didn't help. "You know best? I'll give you my diploma. Tack it on your wall. You be the doctor. I'm out of here."

Anna called from inside the room. "Bella, come here or I'm coming out into the hall."

They both walked back into the room. Anna was standing at the side of the bed, her arms across her chest. She looked at her mother, then Bernstein. "Bella, what are you yelling about?"

"I want you out of here and to the university hospital," Bella stammered.

Jessica turned, looked at Bernie. "Do you agree?"

"No, I don't agree. Bella didn't let me finish. Hodgkin's is a treatable disease, and many cases are curable. I feel she'll be fine, but this is the hard part—she will need another operation. It's called an exploratory, and it involves abdominal surgery. There's no reason a work up has to be done elsewhere."

"Another operation? Why?"

"It's important to see how far the disease has spread. Bella wants her to go to the Bayside Hospital for the procedure. I don't agree with her. Dr. Mortimer is very experienced. I spoke to him last night, and he informed me that he has done over fifteen a year for the last several years—not just for Hodgkin's but other diseases as well. I feel very comfortable that he's doing the surgery."

Jessica looked at Bella. "I've had enough of this. You"—she pointed at her daughter—"dragged her to the quack that gave the antibiotics. I insisted that you see Doctors Mortimer and Bernstein. It's clear they know what to do. Stop being so stubborn."

Bella lowered her voice, her eyes roamed the floor, and she started to cry. "I only want what's best for Anna."

Anna finally had a chance to speak. "Bella, let me listen to Dr. Bernstein without you interfering. I've tried to tell you that I want to be near Grandma, and Dr. Bernie knows what he's doing." She nodded for Bernie to continue.

"In the exploratory, Dr. Mortimer would take specimens from some of the tissues, biopsy the liver and a few lymph nodes in the area. I'll do a bone-marrow biopsy while this is going on. You won't feel a thing since you'll be asleep the whole time." He stopped, took a breath, and looked away from his eleven-year-old patient. "Unfortunately, Dr. Mortimer will have to remove your spleen as part of the procedure."

Bella was the first to speak. "I knew there was more to this. You never mentioned removing her spleen." She choked, and the tears welled up in her eyes. "Bernstein, this seems to be getting more and more complicated by the day. Why the spleen? Aren't there x-ray machines?"

He took out a piece of white paper and drew a rough sketch of the open abdomen. "Here's the liver, the spleen, and some lymph nodes. Dr. Mortimer will biopsy the liver, which will be a small cut, then take a few lymph nodes here, and finally remove the spleen." Bernie stopped to take a drink of water from one of the cups and went on. "The spleen is a big filter of damaged cells and limits any therapy. Besides, it often harbors Hodgkin's disease cells."

Anna looked straight ahead, not saying a word. Bella raised her voice, looking directly at Bernstein. "What are you doing? You know the diagnosis. Why another surgery? Another money-making scheme for doctors?"

Bernstein's faced flushed. He took more deep breaths and again explained that he wanted to know as much as possible before treating the disease. Bella looked at him directly. "You think you can do that here?"

"Bella, I want her to go to Bayside after the exploratory. I don't have a reliable backup once she starts on chemotherapy. That's the time to send her to the big hospital. However, the workup should be done here."

He looked at Bella, Anna, and Jessica again and wondered why he was pushing so hard.

Come on, Bernstein, get out of this mess. Mama wants no part of you. Admit it—you're scared. There'll be a screw up. You'll make a mistake. Stop it, Bernstein. Take care of Anna. You know what you're doing and what's best for this kid. Stay calm. Keep her here. You'll make sure she is safe.

He took deep breaths. *Breathe through the diaphragm, relax...*

Just then, Bob Mortimer walked into the room, went over to Jessica, gave her a hug, and sat at the bedside, smiling at Anna and Bella. "I just received a call from the head nurse that all hell's breaking out here. Anna, are you up to no good again?" His smile broadened.

Bella never let Anna answer. "This guy," she said, pointing at Bernstein, "has been nothing but trouble since you sent him to see my daughter." She started coughing, grabbed a tissue, and expectorated into it. "I want her out of here, and he insists she's better off here."

Mortimer let her calm down, turned to Bernie, and asked if he'd wait at the nurses' station for him. Bernstein complied. While leaving the room, he heard the surgeon ask Bella what happened.

Bernie did as he was told and sat at a desk, staring straight ahead. Mortimer appeared forty-five minutes later. "Bernie, let's get a cup of coffee." Bernstein followed his mentor.

The surgeon took a sip of the coffee before speaking. "You are an excellent doctor with a horrible bedside manner. Everyone's your enemy. You come out swinging, and now it has to stop. I'm not coming to your defense any longer."

Bernie tried to hold his tongue. He respected the surgeon as a physician and a human being. "I'm sorry, Bob. I didn't mean to create a problem. I want to do the best for Anna, and since she's become my patient, I've committed to her."

"You're right—she's better off here—but getting into a shouting match with Bella won't work. I explained to them that you are a pain in the ass, which they already knew. But I picked you because you're as good as anyone at Bayside. But you're like a bulldog once you've taken on a patient; you won't let go."

Bernie blushed and mumbled, "Thank you."

"Here's the deal. You start behaving, apologize to Bella, and you'll continue to care for Anna. I agree with you that she belongs here for the surgery and reassured them that I'm very familiar with this operation. Anna will be safe. Then you can send her to the university for the chemotherapy."

Bernstein had tears in his eyes when he shook the surgeon's hand and went off to apologize, biting his tongue all the way.

Chapter 4

Surgery was delayed for five days. The operating room was busy until Friday, which they rejected and decided to wait until Monday, as the hospital was notoriously short-staffed during weekends.

On that Friday night, Bernie came home, poked at his supper, finally threw his fork on the table, and announced to Leah that he was going for a run. Expert perked up his ears and ran to the door, waiting patiently while Bernie put on his gear. The two made their way to the car. The night air was cold with a strong wind coming in from the north.

He drove to a fenced-in expanse, parked the car near the gate, and saw the tombstones.

A cemetery. How fitting. A deep feeling of loneliness came over him. *I'm on my own with Anna.*

The wind picked up as Bernie ran at a brisk pace, drawing a sweat.

Someone's behind me. I can feel him. He looked back. Tombstones.

With each step of the run, he felt a presence. Running faster didn't help. Realizing that he couldn't keep the pace, he slowed down. Yet the feeling of something chasing him was there.

"Expert! Here, Ex!" Out of the gloom, the dog appeared at his side. They both looked back into darkness. The run ended, Expert jumped into the passenger seat, and Bernie took the wheel and quickly drove home.

Back at the house, the dog ran to his crate, took a gulp of water, shut the door, and closed his eyes.

Ex, you're some protection.

Bernie took a shower and slipped into bed next to Leah, who was half-awake. He tried to get some rest, but it was not to be. He didn't sleep well under the best of circumstances, and he slept worse in times of stress. The dreams were vivid: coffins, shrouds, and images of death.

"Bernie, wake up! You're soaking wet. Stop rolling all over the bed."

"Huh, disease. Oh, sorry," and he tried to go back to sleep. More than once, he had to change his pajamas.

He rolled over to her and said, "These dreams are horrible."

"Do you feel you're doing the right thing for Anna?"

"Yes."

Leah rubbed his shoulders. "Then you should feel good."

He shook his head. "I'm scared."

"Why should you feel frightened? You know what you're doing."

Bernie rubbed his forehead. "Yes, I'm doing the best I can, but I'm afraid of making a mistake—not in the diagnosis, but cancer, like most diseases, has to be taken as the whole patient. Treating cancer patients involves more than knowing what you're doing."

Leah rolled over and looked at him. "What do you mean?"

"I can feel it but can't express it."

She kissed him on the forehead. "Well, you've taken on the responsibility and have done very well. Don't forget that they offered you a position at the medical school. You must be good."

He hugged her tightly, gave her a kiss, and went to sleep.

Chapter 5

Bernstein was in the operating room as part of the team for Anna's surgery early Monday morning. He gave Anna a thumbs-up just before the anesthesia was administered. She smiled and tried to grip his hand. Then out she went.

"Dr. Mortimer, I'm here to do a bone-marrow biopsy on this young lady but also to give you technical assistance if needed." Bernstein had a smirk on his face.

Mortimer made sure that Anna was asleep. "Dr. Bernstein, kiss my ass. You're the only hematologist in the world that gets sick at the sight of blood. I have a crash cart set up just for you." Looking at his operating room nurse, he said, "Nancy, make sure we have enough oxygen for the good Dr. Bernstein. No helium though—his head is big enough."

The surgery went well. Afterward, they took Anna to the intensive care unit as a necessary precaution.

Hours after the procedure, Bernie walked into the unit. The room was large, containing ten beds around a central nursing station. There were three nurses busy taking blood pressures, cleaning wounds, watching for bleeding, and administering medications. The nurses' aides had other responsibilities helping the patients. The head nurse oversaw the entire operation.

The walls were fading white. Overhead lights before 9:00 p.m. were marginally bright. After nine, they became hospital dim. Drapes hung from circular metal supports surrounded most beds. Many patients were attached to respirators singing sad songs of respiratory distress.

He found Anna free of the hardware. She was semiconscious, moaning in pain. He felt her head. It was soaked.

"Hey, kid, how you doing?" he said while looking at her chart.

"I hurt. The pain medicine isn't helping me." She started to cry.

Bernstein puffed up his chest, his face reddened, and he started to bite his tongue. He turned and bolted to the nursing station, where he grabbed the head nurse by the arm.

"Jan, what the hell are you doing? I have a patient in pain. The last dose of morphine was given almost four hours ago." He slammed the chart on her desk. "Can't you read? The order calls for two milligrams of morphine as needed. That means as needed, not every four hours, you schmuck."

She looked at him. "Don't you tell us what to do. This child will get addicted—or worse, killed—by your sloppy order. I'll not have my nurses responsible for your incompetence. 'Give morphine as needed.' That's criminal."

Bernie bit his tongue. "You're an idiot. I'm the one giving the orders, and it's my ass on the line. If Anna's awake enough to have pain, she's awake enough to have the medication." Biting his tongue didn't help. He stepped forward until he was only a foot in front of her face. "Morphine has to be given before pain gets too severe. Wait too long, and it won't work. Now stop jerking off and give me a syringe with two milligrams of morphine."

Bernstein hadn't finished. "You have no business in an intensive care unit. Get your fat ass out of here."

The nurse reluctantly drew up the medicine and gave it to Bernie. "Here, you give it," she snapped. "You'll be responsible."

Bernie took the syringe and slowly injected the morphine. He stayed in the unit, gabbed with a few of the nurses, and waited. Anna was still in pain ten minutes later. Bernie gave her another shot. Slowly the girl relaxed and went to sleep.

He took a deep breath and then another and started to relax. "I'm not going anywhere for the next two hours. I'll be back, and Anna better not be in pain."

As he left the unit, he heard Jan say to no one, "I'm going to report that guy."

On the way out, he bumped into Bella, who had been standing at the threshold of the room. She squeezed his hand and said, "Thank you."

Bernie did his best not to faint.

Chapter 6

Once Anna was out of the ICU, Bernie stopped by twice a day. About a week after the surgery, he made his usual stop and asked, "Jessica, how's Anna doing? Anything new?"

She pulled him aside and whispered that she was concerned about an infection. "Bernie, the wound seems to be seeping pus. Anna can't hold any fluids, and she complains of abdominal pain. Don't you think she should be healing a little faster by this time?"

He agreed and headed into Anna's room. Once inside, Bernie nodded to Bella, gave Anna a hug, and asked, "How are you feelin'?" while looking at the chart.

Anna had lost weight, giving her a thin and pale look. "I feel terrible," she said and turned away.

He asked Anna to lie flat in bed and examined her belly. "You're bloated. Are you in pain?"

Anna barely looked at him. "I feel full all the time. Look at my stomach. It's like a round ball."

Bernie scratched his forehead. "Your bowel sounds are very quiet—in fact, too quiet." He pointed at her abdomen. "You should be up and about by this time." He scratched his earlobe.

"On top of that, you have an infection at the wound site. I'm going to put you on antibiotics."

Anna started to cry. "I miss Earl. I want Earl."

Bernie was puzzled. "Who's Earl?"

Bella answered, "Her puppy... They are inseparable. He sleeps with her."

Jessica, standing near the bed, asked, "Bernie, do you think that missing someone could affect her health?"

He shrugged. "Jessica, anything is possible. I've read a few medical papers describing so-called alternative medical treatments including one that used dog therapy on the elderly. It seemed to work." He threw his arms outward. "So where's the puppy?"

Jessica responded first. "Bernie, we can't bring a puppy into the hospital."

He shook his head. "Look, what the hell do we have to lose? Bring me the puppy. I'll get him in."

The next day Earl arrived at the hospital through the doctor's lounge.

Holy shit—sixty pounds of Doberman.

I hate Dobermans. Puppy, my ass.

The feeling was mutual. Earl didn't like Bernstein either. The dog peed, struggled, and bit the doctor.

You are a miserable excuse for a dog. Probably a junkyard breeding.

41

Earl tore at his shirt.

"Dr. Bernstein, get that animal out of here," yelled a floor nurse as she tried to stop them.

Earl showed his teeth. Bernstein growled. Earl squirmed away and started sniffing the rooms.

"Oh my God, a dog," rang through the hospital floor.

Not to be daunted, Earl was into the hunt. He was looking for Anna, and there was no turning back. Bernstein caught the dog again. Another battle ensued.

"Screw you."

Shirt torn, arm bleeding, he dumped Earl into the room. Silence, then squealing, followed by Anna's crying.

Bernstein looked at Bella. She was laughing. Tears flowed down her cheeks. Everyone joined her.

Anna made a quick recovery from that point on.

And Bernie could only pull on his ear.

Chapter 7

Each day before the slides were ready, Bernie came around at lunchtime with sandwiches. True to her word, Toni had fresh coffee ready. He tiptoed into the room, came up behind her, and kissed her on the back of the neck.

"I'll give you a half hour to cut that out, Bernie," she said with a laugh. They'd then get down to work looking at slides or chat if there was nothing else to do. She was a carnivore and he a vegetarian, so they had small differences in taste. Toni had the double cheeseburger, he the double hummus on pita with a side order of tabbouleh.

"Bernie, why don't you eat meat?"

He thought for a few moments while munching. "You know, I thought about it, then decided there was enough killing in the world. I didn't need to eat animals to survive. But I do eat fish occasionally. It doesn't seem to bother me."

Toni took another big bite and shrugged.

"Besides," he continued, "when I was in med school, I did research on bovine cartilage."

"What does that have to do with it?"

"I had to get the cartilage I needed from a slaughterhouse. While waiting, I could hear the animals crying before the killing. That pretty much ended my interest in meat."

She looked at her sandwich, made a face, and threw the rest in the garbage.

He laughed. "Try some hummus?"

They shared the rest of his lunch, and Toni brought up the subject of the dog. "I can't believe you brought a dog into the hospital and got away with it. What made you do it?"

He shrugged. "I don't really know. It just seemed like the right thing to do. Anna wasn't getting better—in fact, a little worse. I thought it would perk her up."

Toni took a stab at the tabbouleh. "Well, the news is all over the hospital. Bernstein might be a human being after all."

He smiled. "Ah, shit, one ounce of kindness and my reputation is destroyed."

She shook her head. "No, Bernie, your patient got better quickly. Maybe there's more to medicine than the books tell us."

He took a big bite of hummus and shrugged.

Four days after surgery, the slides were ready for viewing. There were abnormal cells in many of the lymph nodes, but the spleen appeared normal. Bernie felt the slides depicted Hodgkin's, but Toni remained cautious. "I don't know, Bernie. I just can't call it without seeing Reed-Sternberg cells."

He nodded. "I understand, but there are so many small changes that when added up, I feel she must have Hodgkin's."

"Bernie, you are an excellent histopathologist and see things under slides that most of the pathologists miss. Wait a few more minutes." She continued to look. "I see the changes. They are subtle but definite. I'll buy it. It's Hodgkin's."

Bernie rubbed his forehead. "Yep, this shows that the disease has spread from one set of nodes to the next—typical of Hodgkin's, not lymphomas."

A week later, Anna was ready to be transferred to Bayside Medical Center.

Bernie was at peace. To Bella and Jessica, he said, "She'll be cared for by one of the best men in the country. He wrote the book on Hodgkin's." There were smiles all around—especially from Bella.

Referral. Hallelujah!

A snowstorm raged as he headed home. His good feeling had left him, and he felt an ominous chill.

Chapter 8

In mid-December, as the sun drifted down and green-gray streaks appeared on the horizon, news of Anna came back. Bernie stopped at the nurses' station and asked Jessica, "How's Anna doing?"

"Bernie, they feel she has a lymphoma. She was misdiagnosed."

He turned pale. The room started to spin, and he sat down.

Oh my God! I put her through surgery for nothing.

"Jessica, I was so sure she had Hodgkin's. Holy shit. I can't believe it. How could I be so wrong?" The knife cut deep. "Jess, I… I went over those slides very carefully. We're certain she has Hodgkin's. I don't know…"

She looked at him, her eyes filled with tears.

"No one blames you. The doctors said it was a difficult diagnostic problem. They had to send the slides to the Bethesda Naval Hospital for final diagnosis. Apparently, everyone had the same problem. In the end most of the doctors felt it was a lymphoma; others agreed with you that it was Hodgkin's."

Bernstein grabbed the chair and held on. The room kept spinning.

"Bernie, we feel she had good care here. Even Bella calmed down, and poor Anna wants to come home."

The fact that the slides had to be sent to Bethesda, the top diagnostic pathology center in the country, didn't satisfy him. He ran straight to Toni's office.

"Toni, we have to review the slides on Anna. They think it's a lymphoma."

Toni yelled for the laboratory tech to bring Anna's remaining slides. "That's bullshit. We went over them better than they could."

Bernie couldn't stop pacing. "Where did we go wrong?"

Toni sprang up, grabbing his arm. "Bernie, stop it. We both thought it was Hodgkin's."

Together they spent another hour carefully reviewing the slides.

Toni broke the silence. "I still believe it's Hodgkin's."

"Toni, Toni…" Tears filled his eyes, and he walked out of her office. Bernstein now was a blind man walking in a fog. Turning right, he walked into the morgue. It was cold, gray, and sterile. He slammed his fist against the wall and screamed like a dying animal.

Eventually Bernstein emerged, stumbled to his car, and drove slowly to the office.

His eyes were red and heavy, full of tears. He finished his day in slow motion.

Chapter 9

The bad news didn't stop.

"Anna's lost more weight."

"She stopped eating."

"Her fever's back."

Whatever therapy they tried didn't work, and so it went.

"Anna's in constant pain."

"They stopped the chemotherapy. They're giving her radiation."

Stop… Stop. I don't want to hear anymore.

The winter storms continued, relentlessly closing roads, icing trees, and breaking power lines.

Bernstein arrived home late one evening. The boys were in bed; Russell and Leah sat in the living room. The fire in the fireplace was burning low, embers red.

Leah came over to give him a hug. Russell threw him a kiss from his chair. He had been living with them for more than two months. The German shepherd dog shows were infrequent during the winter. And there was no sign of Rob making amends with his lover.

Bernie dragged himself to a soft chair and collapsed into it. "I feel like crap. I can't believe I was so wrong about Anna."

Leah looked him in the eye. "Stop the whining. You've been at it for weeks. Have your patients been abandoning you? I'd imagine they would, since you're so lousy."

"No, my practice is growing. It doesn't make sense."

Russell pulled himself up and put his arm around Bernie. "Maybe you're not so bad. Did you ever think you might expect too much from yourself?"

Bernie gave his friend a hug and thanked him.

Russell smiled. "Well, daahling, let's have dinner. I've been cooking all day for you. We're tired of watching you crying in your soup."

Leah pushed Bernie into his seat, and the family joined him.

Chapter 10

As usual, January's weather was lousy. Bernie sat with Toni during lunch.

"Bernie, you're walking around like a bloodhound. Is it still Anna?"

"Afraid so. I can't get it out of my mind that I hurt the kid. That surgery was terrible. She could have died."

"Bernstein, get over it. Mistakes happen. Besides, if it was wrong, we were both wrong; but I don't think so. If they're so right, why aren't they helping her?"

"I don't know, Toni. It could be a resistant lymphoma."

"Yes, it could be Hodgkin's or a lymphoma, both resistant. We did our best. Stop being a big pain in the ass. I'll tell you this—we know what we're doing, and we'll have to go on from here."

Bernie rubbed his forehead. "It's all bullshit. Chemotherapy destroys the body—cancer cells along with normal tissue. Most patients die. When they live, who knows why? When they die, well, it's the cancer. Shit. It's all a waste of time."

Toni stopped eating and looked directly into his eyes. "So you think everything you do is all for nothing?"

"Yes. I feel like a pawn on a gigantic chessboard and follow the commands of a stranger's hand. Look what happens—an innocent kid is hurt."

He stopped, took the pink ball out of his pocket, and started bouncing it at his feet. "What I'm trying to say is that there are treatment plans that oncologists follow. Generally, we use the same drugs for the same types of cancers."

"Stop bouncing that stupid ball and get to the point," Toni yelled.

He held the ball and went on. "If therapy works, we're heroes; if it fails, we're sadists. But we have no idea why one treatment works and another doesn't."

"You're full of crap. There is logic to your work. Suppose you did nothing? What would have happened?"

"She'd not have had that surgery, that's for sure." He started to pace around the room, reached into his pocket, and out came the pink ball again. Bernie wasn't finished. "But Toni, think of my other point. Why does one patient live and the other die with the same treatment, the same supposed cancer?"

"You're off base, Bernie. We're in the infancy of cancer research. There will be a day when each cancer will have its own label. Treatments will be tailored to individuals."

"Toni, I have to live with the fact that I don't know what I'm doing. I don't understand this disease; most likely, no one else does either. To make matters worse, Anna winds up with big-time surgery. That's the part that hurts the most."

She grabbed a pickle off his plate, munched on half, and put it back. "With or without the surgery, she'd still be in the same place. No response to therapy."

He nodded and finished off the pickle.

"Bernie, there is something that you did with Anna that's been told all over the hospital. It was your relationship with her. Even bringing in that dog. That's the human touch that I think makes a difference in therapy. Try to remember how well she did under your care."

"Come on, Toni. I didn't give her chemotherapy. I fucked up the diagnosis, remember?"

"Bernie, you're so bright and yet you don't see how important it is to do that little something that brings a better outlook. You have it in you. Let it out. Scientists don't know enough of how the body works. I think that's the unknown."

He looked at her. "What unknown? Sounds like bullshit to me."

She looked into his eyes, and he turned away. "No, Bernie, it's not bullshit. Think about it." Toni tried to smile. Instead, her lips just pressed together. "Bernie, let me tell you what I've learned. Life is a wheel. Don't get too excited when you're on top. And don't get too crushed when you're on the bottom. The wheel turns."

He shrugged, wrapped up the remains of their lunch, and tossed all of it in the trash.

He nodded. "I'll see you tomorrow," he said and left her office.

Chapter 11

A few days later, Maria, his secretary, walked into his office through the open door. "Doctor, Susan Ferreira called while you were seeing Mr. Williams. She wanted to remind you not to eat before coming over to see Joe. She has a special meal cooked for the three of you."

Bernie made a face. "That woman is going to drive me nuts. After I see her husband, she makes a chorizo dish with onions, peppers, and some kind of homemade tomato sauce on a Portuguese roll. She knows I'm a vegetarian."

"Why don't you refuse?"

"Did you ever try to reason with a Portuguese woman when it comes to food? Forget it. She claims the sausage is good for me. Besides, I don't want to insult her." He hesitated for a moment and added, "It's too good."

He called home before leaving the office. Russell answered. "Daahling, how are you? Do you feel better today?"

"Yes, a little better." He didn't feel the need to go into detail. "I'll be home a little late. I have to see a homebound patient of mine. Don't hold supper for me. I'll eat out."

"Oh, you're such a poop. I planned to make a special cheer-up-Bernie supper. Now you've spoiled it. Well, be like that, but I don't want you coming home drunk. If you do, I'll be very upset."

"Yes, dear," he muttered.

Bernstein made his usual stop to pick up a six-pack of Portuguese beer, Joe Ferreira's favorite, and then a dozen donuts. From there, he was off to the Ferreiras. Susan greeted him, and Joe, lying on his back, head elevated, stuck out his hand for a shake.

"Come on, doc, we gotta talk about the trade the Red Sox made today."

"Hey, Joe, get over it. The Sox aren't going to win a thing until they get over the curse of the Bambino."

"Damn New Yorkers—you're spoiled."

They both laughed.

"Susan, bring in the chorizo," yelled Joe.

"Oh, be quiet. What do think I'm doing, you cripple?"

Joe shook his head. "See, she gives me no respect."

He had cancer of the prostate that had spread to his spinal cord. Joe Ferreira was crippled from the waist down.

Bernstein examined Joe. "There's no change, and the paralysis isn't going to get better. I'm sorry."

"Hey, doc, it's not your fault. It's the way things are. Let's eat."

Susan brought in the food, beer, and donuts. They ate slowly, talking about this, that, and everything. When they were finished, Bernstein wrote the prescriptions and headed home.

Fuck this. What good am I? I should have been a social worker.

He stopped off at a liquor store along the way.

Chapter 12

Bernie avoided Jessica's floor as much as possible. It didn't work. He had to ask.

"Bernie, Anna is not getting better. In fact, she's worse. They're planning on sending her home. The radiation treatments failed."

Bernstein stopped asking and started driving his sports car through the winding roads at night, the ever-present bottle at his side.

I wonder how close I can get to that tree. Somehow, he missed. *Alcohol ain't so bad.*

Two nights later, he lost control of his car. The police found him, an empty whiskey bottle at his side. They brought him home. No charges were filed. Leah and Russell carried him up the stairs and laid him on the sofa. She'd talk to him in the morning.

Early the next day, Russell took the boys to school and left for the day.

When he woke, Bernie ran to the bathroom and vomited. His head was pounding. "Where's the Percocet? I'm sick."

"I threw your fucking pills out with the alcohol. They're in the sewer. Go join them."

"What happened to me? How did I get home?"

"The police brought you. You were stupid drunk, and I want you out of the house." She pointed to a large overnight bag in the hall. "You're ruining this family and killing yourself." She started hitting him, crying and screaming loudly.

Bernstein looked at Leah, took her blows, and tried to hold her. "You don't mean…" and he started to cry.

His tears turned to heaving, and when he couldn't control himself any longer, he fell to his knees, grabbing her legs.

"You're nothing but a drunk and an addict. You've become a pathetic son of a bitch." She looked at him, bent down, and joined her husband on the floor. "Please, Bernie, you're too precious to me. Stop the drinking. It's your ego that's in the way. Stop tripping over it."

They lay clutching each other and crying. He made his promises. This time he'd get help. "I'll make an appointment to see a psychiatrist and go to AA."

"You're like all the drunks. Nothing but promises. Bernie, there won't be any other chances. I'm going to the AA meetings with you, like it or not."

He nodded his acceptance.

They lay there for some time, finally curling into each other. Leah whispered that the boys were at school and Russell was off looking at a new litter of puppies.

He ran his hand over her body, and they responded to each other; the loneliness of the months was lost in love. Afterward, Bernie held onto Leah. "Wow, drinking has benefits."

Leah nibbled his neck. "Never again, if you don't stop."

Chapter 13

The next morning, Russell called from the kitchen, "Bernie, come on, darling, time for breakfast."

"Coming, Russell. What's cooking?"

"I made a special omelet. My poor doctor has been so depressed, I decided to make the queen of omelets—eggs, a small dollop of heavy cream, cream cheese, and smoked salmon. I made one for everyone in the family." A smile that would have melted the coldest heart flowed from his lips.

Bernstein scowled and mumbled something about cholesterol.

"Oh, Bernie, don't be a stick in the mud. I slaved all morning for you. Now, let's have a good breakfast."

It was delicious.

After eating, Bernstein looked around. "What was that noise?"

Russell looked about. "What noise?"

"My arteries closing."

"Oh, Bernie, just stop that. It was a burp."

"Now remember, Russell, today's your annual physical. I expect you there by 3:00 p.m. Not late as usual. Otherwise, no rectal exam."

"Dr. Bernstein, the children are here."

The boys and Bernie laughed. Leah joined in and finally Russell.

Chapter 14

Two weeks later, Bernstein had a new patient. He walked into the examining room and found Bella. His mouth fell open.

"Dr. Bernstein, sit."

He sat.

"Stop staring at me and close your mouth. I'm here for a physical. Aren't you capable of handling medical problems?"

He nodded. "Ah, ah, yes."

"I have high blood pressure. I want you to take care of me."

"Bella, I'd be glad to take care of you, but I assumed that you'd have nothing to with me. I'm very upset about Anna's diagnosis."

"That's not your fault. Anna's getting worse and wants to come home. She told them about Earl and how you just walked the dog into the hospital while all the nurses screamed. The doctors think she's making it up or you're nuts."

Bernstein smiled. "The doctors are probably right."

"No, Bernie, you were right. She received better care here."

He mumbled his thanks but insisted that Anna was at the best hospital. "They'll come up with something." *Yeah, a miracle, and they're in short supply.*

He examined her. Her blood pressure was high, but otherwise the exam was normal. He smelled the odor of wine.

"Bella, the first step would be to stop drinking. It's making your blood pressure go up." He sat down and went into a lecture about blood pressure and the side effects. "You can't afford two sick patients in the same house. I'll recheck the pressure in a few weeks. Now it's up to you to stop."

She looked at Bernstein. "You think I should stop drinking? And you?"

He turned red. *How did she know?* Bella had read his mind.

"Bernie, did you think in a small town no one would know that the police had to bring you home? Especially when you wound up on the mayor's porch."

"What's wrong with that? He invited me."

"You were in your car."

"Oh. You got a point there."

He shook his head. "I've been going to AA meetings. The first one scared the crap out of me, but I found the members to be pleasant and supportive."

Bella nodded. She understood. "I guess they've all been in the same boat."

"I'm going tonight. Why not come?"

She agreed. He'd pick her up at seven.

On the way out of the office, he gave her a list of the AA meetings in the area and then headed home.

Chapter 15

It was a lousy winter—snow every few days, sleet, icy roads, and the usual short daylight hours. Most New Englanders were fed up and ready for spring, but being ready wouldn't make it come any sooner. Mother Nature wasn't ready to relent—not that early. She had more in store.

After work, Bernie jumped into his Jeep, took a deep breath, and headed to the Whitestones' home. He parked in the driveway. The house had been built in the 1870s. It was made of wood, both the sides and the roof. The front of the house had a fence made out of posts tied together with wire. The walkway led from the driveway toward the house. On either side stood low-growing evergreens. As usual, Bernstein knocked, didn't wait for an answer, and walked in.

Their daughter, Jo Adams, was usually there busying herself about her mother. "Here, Ma, take some homemade soup. Take some pasta—I just made it for you."

Marge would munch half a mouthful and turn away.

When he was alone with her, it was always the same. She insisted she had caused the cancer but never spoke more. She would turn away from him in silence and stare at the wall. Each house call ended the same.

Damn, I can't understand it. She's still alive.

Chapter 16

He didn't hear anything more regarding Anna for several weeks. Finally, Bob Mortimer called Bernie to inform him that Anna was back in the community hospital.

"We received her records with a final note that she was terminal. Comfort measures only."

"Bob, what the hell am I supposed to do? I've been wrong all along. Besides, I'm sure they hit the kid with everything."

"Bernie, Bella is demanding you see Anna today. By the way, she punched one of the doctors when he told her there wasn't any hope for her daughter."

"Did she really punch him?"

"Bernie, stop fighting. Go see Anna. She is terminal and needs blood. I won't give it to her. I won't prolong her life. Bella and Jessica are insisting that you take care of her. I've transferred her to your care." He took a deep breath and went on. "Yes, she did punch him in the face—the nose, to be exact. Broke it too."

Bernstein knew how difficult it was for this surgeon to give up. "I'll see her tonight."

An ice storm covered the roads as Bernstein drove to the hospital to see Anna. He felt as if he was driving on a skating rink, and he was the only performer. The Jeep skidded, slipped into a snow bank, recovered, and drove itself the rest of the way.

Once there, he went straight to her room. He was prepared for the worst but found her beyond that. Anna was curled into a ball. Skin rested on bone, a skeleton with expressionless eyes awaiting death. Her breaths came slowly, then increased, slowed down, and stopped.

She's dead.

He felt for a pulse.

"Hi, Dr. Bernie... guess I don't look so good?"

He recovered. "Nah, kid, you just caught me by surprise." Bernie gave Anna a gentle hug. Anything harder, and she'd break.

She told about her adventure in Boston and finished with Bella punching the doctor. "Gave him a bloody nose too."

The new problem was major stomach pains along with severe emaciation. Anna had taken only small amounts of liquids over the last few weeks. An IV of saline dripped into her vein, providing enough fluids to keep her alive.

"Dr. Bernie, I haven't gone to the bathroom, like number two, in a long time."

Bernstein shook his head. "The plumbing won't work unless something goes down the other end."

Tears came to her eyes. "It hurts too much. I know you'll fix it... won't you?"

He hesitated, looked for a hole to crawl into, and found none.

I can't lie to a patient, eleven-year-old or not.

"Of course I will. A piece of cake—might take a few days," he lied.

She smiled a big smile and squeezed his hand.

Bernstein told Anna that he'd speak to Jessica and Bella and then be back.

They were in the family room. Bella rose to her full height. "Bernie, we want her treated."

"No way. You're asking for a miracle, and I'm fresh out. They're right in Boston—keep her comfortable." He winced, awaiting a punch.

"Bernie, if nothing is done she'll die within weeks." Bella was not budging, and Jessica nodded in agreement.

"Look, I went over her Boston records, and the treatments didn't touch her. They used all the drugs available for lymphoma. Anything else would be experimental. On top of that, she's so malnourished that additional chemotherapy would kill her."

He stopped and started pacing about the room, pulled out his Spalding, bounced it on the floor, and then cradled it in his hand. "I'd be the executioner."

Shit, I'm getting nowhere. Another killing. This kid will die, and I'll be in charge. Go to hell, all of you.

He withdrew into a chair, sweating, and stared blankly at the two women.

They waited for his response. It took time.

Bernie shook his head. "Look, I thought this was Hodgkin's disease. The professors felt differently. I was wrong." He shrugged and then went on. "It's hard to imagine that the guys in Boston made a mistake."

Bella put her hand on his shoulder. "Bernie, maybe you are right."

He looked at her. "In Hodgkin's there are special cells called Reed-Sternberg cells. They make the diagnosis along with other changes. We didn't see those typical cells; nor did the Boston group. But I saw changes in the tissue…"

His pager suddenly rang, and he excused himself to find a phone. It was Leah.

"The roads are pure ice. You're to stay at the hospital tonight." It was an order, and Bernie "yes dear"-ed and promised not to leave. He returned to the women, told them about the road conditions, and found beds that they could sleep in for the night.

"Let me think about it, and we'll talk in the morning. Meanwhile I'm going to the laboratory." And off he went.

Chapter 17

"Hey John, wake up. I want Anna Bing's slides." After much grumbling on the tech's part, he brought the slides. Bernstein found a microscope and a pot of coffee and settled in for a long night. He prayed, bargaining his soul to anyone who would listen, including the devil. After hours of negotiations with his inner being, he found them.

Shit. These are Reed-Sternberg cells.

He looked again, stood up, walked around the room, came back, and looked at the corner of the slides.

I can't believe it. How'd we miss them? Typical Reed-Sternberg.

All the surgery, pain, and fear that Anna went through had been necessary. Bernstein put his head on the desk and cried. He cried for the girl, for himself, and for the futility of treating cancer.

My God. Maybe I can make a difference. Now what do I do?

A voice behind him whispered, "That's your problem. You owe me."

He turned. No one was there.

Bernstein took a deep breath, looked at the slides one more time, and marked the important areas. He was asleep in minutes.

Chapter 18

Toni found Bernstein at her desk in the morning drinking coffee and staring into the microscope. He turned to see the cause of the noise. "Shit, about time you came in. Here, have some coffee and look at this."

"Can I take off my coat? What's the big deal?"

Toni grabbed his cup, took a sip. "My God, this is cold. How can you drink this crap?"

"Forget the coffee. Look." He moved over, and she sat next to him. It took a few minutes. Toni moved the slides slowly and then looked at him.

"These are Reed-Sternberg cells. Are they Anna's slides?"

"This is such a small area of abnormal cells. No wonder we missed them," Toni said, shaking her head.

He nodded. They looked at each other, hugged, screamed, and hugged again. "I've got to see the family immediately."

"Bernie, slow down. What can you do?"

"I have no idea, but at least it's a start."

He ran to their room. The three were sitting together. Jessica and Bella were asleep. Anna lay on the bed, pillow clutched against her abdomen, tears in her eyes.

"Anna has Hodgkin's. We're sure of it."

That woke the ladies. For a short time they were quiet. Then Bella cried and Jessica joined her. Anna looked straight ahead.

"When are you going to start treatment?" cried Bella.

"Whoa. Slow down. I need time to think about it. I'll be back later in the day." He kissed Anna on the forehead and left for his office.

When he arrived, Maria was waiting for him. "Dr. Bernstein, most of the patients canceled; the roads are too icy. I fit them in tomorrow. Is that all right?"

He looked at her. "Don't we have a full schedule? How could you put more patients in?"

Maria looked at him with her big brown eyes. "Well, what did you want me to do? They have to see you. We'll just work late."

All she heard were unintelligible screams as he slammed the door to his office.

Due to the weather, the schedule was indeed light. He went home early but not before notifying the floor nurse that he'd see Anna in the morning.

Chapter 19

The house was warm, with logs burning in the fireplace and supper on the table. He kept quiet most of the evening. Just before bedtime, Bernstein started pacing.

"Honey, I'm taking Expert skiing."

"Are you nuts? It's almost midnight, and there's a foot of snow out there. Besides, Expert might get sick."

"He'll be fine. The golf course shouldn't be crowded. Won't have to wait for a tee time. I have to unwind."

"Be careful."

The dog pounced for the door as soon as he heard the word *skiing*. They piled into the car and drove to the golf course.

Great, it's empty.

Bernstein turned to the dog. "Ex, you're a lot smarter than I am. I need your help."

He received a sympathetic lick; then the dog jumped out of the car and into the fresh snow. Bernie followed. It was a full moon.

"A perfect time to think, old boy." He explained the problem to Expert. "The kid has Hodgkin's disease, and I need four drugs to treat her. Any ideas?"

Bernie looked into the dog's eyes. Expert pondered the dilemma.

Bernstein said, "There are a few combinations of drugs they didn't use, thinking that she had a lymphoma. Maybe there's the solution."

He made tracks in the snow with his skis while Expert ran alongside at a steady gait.

"You see, Ex, for some reason four drugs work better in Hodgkin's than three." He went over the treatments she had received, mumbling, remembering what had been used and what hadn't. "I can make a mix out of three. Need one more, and it has got to be good. We have only one chance with this kid."

Expert suddenly stopped and stared into the night sky. The hair on the nape of his neck stood straight up. A loud boom interrupted the night. Bernie looked up into moonlight.

That's funny—no jet stream. "My life is getting spookier by the day," he said aloud. *It's the devil, come to collect the rent. Can't be! Screw the devil...* "Ex, we're on the right track. You did good, old boy." That got him a wag.

He skied toward a light in the darkness. The dog followed.

Chapter 20

Early the next morning he drove to the hospital. Bernstein's face was puffy; dark rings encircling his red eyes. Jessica and Bella were camped out by Anna's bed; she was fast asleep. He motioned for both to follow him into the library, which they did.

"As I told you yesterday, Anna has Hodgkin's." He cleared his throat. "But I only have part of a plan. I need another drug. In my mind, she needs four drugs that would act on the cancer cells. So far I've come up with three that haven't been used on Anna."

They both smiled and then caught themselves as he went on.

"We can't try half a treatment. It won't work. We have to think of another drug and hope it'll be the right one."

His brain wouldn't keep still. *Maybe, just maybe.*

Bella looked at him. "Bernie, I know you have an idea. Go ahead. You can try something else the next time."

Bernstein moved forward, his face red. "Damn it, don't you get it? There won't be a next time. We have one chance—that's it."

Both women shifted back in their chairs and kept quiet.

He took a few deep breaths and shouted, "The drugs take three weeks or more to work while we pray that they do some good and don't kill her. If she survives that first month, we get to do it all over again, repeating the same horrible scene. All this with an eleven-year-old that has no idea of the torture she's about to go through."

He bit his lip out of frustration. "Anna isn't getting a second chance if the medicines don't work the first time. Take off your blinders."

Crap! Why am I getting pissed at them? He cooled down, started to apologize and then stopped. *Screw it. Let them believe what they want.*

Meanwhile the committee in Bernstein's head decided to hold a meeting. *Use the three drugs. No one can blame you for not trying.*

Don't listen. You'll never be able to live with yourself.

That's nuts. Use the three. It's the safe way out.

Bernie wants something that'll work, not something that's safe.

Schmuck. For once, do the sensible thing.

There has to be a better way. Keep looking.

The women moved back. Bella asked if he was all right. Bernstein stayed mute.

He heard Jessica whisper to her daughter, "He gets like that. I've seen it before."

Bernie finally left the committee meeting. "Let's see Anna." He led the way. Bella was right behind, and Jessica followed.

Anna had been given two units of blood during the night. Color had returned to her cheeks.

"What kind of blood did you give me? I feel a lot better."

The ladies smiled. Bernstein could only think of the short-term benefit of a transfusion.

It works until you need more or make your own… That'll be the day.

"Anna, it's Willis Reed's blood. It doesn't come any better than that."

"Who's Willis Reed?"

"He's *The Captain*. Just trust me." Bernstein grabbed a piece of paper from the night table, folded it into a ball, and took a hook shot into the garbage can. "Two points for the captain."

They all laughed but had no idea why.

Anna looked at him, a twinkle in her eye. "You do pretty good for a correspondence-school graduate."

Bernie took a bow.

Anna tried smiling. "I knew you were right. But what took you so long?"

"I was late paying the electric bill. They cut off my microscope light." He received a smirk in return.

They chatted a bit longer, but it was time to excuse himself and complete hospital rounds. While doing so, he came across Donna, the head nurse in charge of the day shift.

"Dr. Bernstein, are you all right? You haven't been yelling at the nurses for over a week."

"Me, yelling? Perish the thought." As he spoke, his arm went around her back and pulled her bra.

"You're a bad boy," she said while slapping his butt.

"Okay, Donna, I'm heading home. Anything happens, give me a call."

Bernstein drove home slowly, sipping a Coke and thinking about Anna. As soon as he opened the door, Leah greeted him. "You better be home on time tomorrow. It's the first night of Passover. Our parents are coming for the Seder."

"Passover? Are we celebrating early?"

"No. It's just that you've been in a fog for a few weeks."

"Wow." He sat down. Leah came over, rubbed his head, and gave him a kiss.

"How's Anna?"

"She's the same. I'm trying to come up with a regimen. So far, no luck."

"Honey, I know you'll do the right thing."

Russell nodded in agreement. "Okay, time to eat." With that, Russell and Leah headed to the kitchen.

I wish I felt as confident.

Chapter 21

The following night Bernie arrived home on time. He came in from the lower floor and climbed the steps to the family room where Quinella sat growling at a TV commercial featuring Lassie jumping fences to help some kid. Molly, Leah's mother, stood next to the sofa, commenting about the stupid dog barking at a television program. Her husband, Alvin, was standing nearby. David and Mark were halfway up a fireman's pole in the same room.

David, who was upside-down climbing the pole, laughed. "She barks at commercials, especially Lassie. Quinella doesn't like anyone interfering with Walter Cronkite."

The German shepherd continued growling but turned her head toward Molly. The woman got the message and took a hasty retreat to a corner of the room, muttering about the dumb dog. She ignored Bernie as her nose searched the ceiling.

The two boys came down the pole, gave Bernie a kiss on each cheek. "How did the day go?" he asked.

They both nodded.

"Ah… Dad?" He turned to find Allan and Jack with their backs against the wall.

"Okay, what happened?"

They slowly moved away from the wall, exposing a large hole. "Jack made a good tackle. We'll help you fix it in the morning."

He gave them both kisses on the cheek. "Not a problem. We're getting good at home repairs, especially wall boards."

He found Leah and Russell in the kitchen with his own mother, Sally, directing the Seder meal. Russell insisted that he knew how to make kugel. "After all, Sally, I'm part Amish. We invented kugel. It's simply noodles and cottage cheese."

Sally was decorated in her holiday finest—bright red hair due to an overdose of henna and lipstick brighter than the hair. "Yes, Russell, but you don't know shit about kosher and less about Passover. So shut your effin' mouth or I'll forget I'm a lady."

"Sally, you're over eighty. The kids will pick up your language," barked Molly, who had now wandered into the kitchen.

Here's trouble, thought Bernie as he watched his mother turn toward Molly, fire in her eyes.

"Hi, Sally," he said and ran over to give her a kiss.

"My son is here. Look, everyone, the doctor is here." She got him in a bear hug, letting go only when he wheezed.

Overhearing the commotion, his father, Harry, came in from the other room and gave his son a kiss on both cheeks. "Bernie, you look tired. Let's all have a glass of Schlivovitz to start the holiday. Alvin, boys, come here for some plum brandy. It's Passover."

"Harry, no! The boys are too young. That stuff's dynamite," said Sally as she held out her glass.

"Let's drink to everyone's health and long life."

They all raised their cups and drank. The boys tasted, coughed, and turned red.

"Welcome to Passover," said Harry.

Bernie took a sip and gave the rest to Leah. "You know what I find so mystical? The Hebrew calendar is a based on the moon. So every first night of Passover there's a full moon. Three thousand years of it." He stopped for a moment and then ushered everyone outside. The night was cloudless, and the stars were lost in the brightness of the moon.

Molly broke the reverie by announcing that the Jewish Mafia— her name for the boys—had put a hole in the wall, a dog was sitting on the couch barking at the television, and a raccoon was chasing the cats around the house. "You're all nuts," she added.

They ignored her.

The commotion continued until the raccoon tired and laid down next to the cats, the dogs went to sleep, and Quinella settled in to watch Cronkite in peace. Sally stopped screaming at Russell. It was time for the Seder to begin.

They sat down. Harry picked up a Haggadah; a copy was sitting in front of each place setting. Pointing to the front cover, Harry started the service. "This book tells the story of Passover, which is the Exodus of the Hebrews from Egypt. Our forefathers went from slavery to freedom over three thousand years ago. This holiday is for all people still in slavery waiting to be free."

They thanked God for the blessing of the fruit of the vine while drinking the first glass of wine. Bernstein gave his to Leah.

Bernie's thoughts were of those held hostage to disease, while Harry spoke of slavery everywhere. Pointing to the Passover plate, which contained various symbolic foods, Harry continued, "Every civilization contributed to the Seder. But the Romans had the greatest input. Especially the orgies."

He stopped, took another drink of wine, winked at Sally, and commented that this was the time of year to plant seeds.

"Harry!" screamed Sally.

Bernie suggested to David that he read the four questions.

"Come on, David. The youngest has to read. These four questions have to be answered. They explain the meaning of Passover. Then we can eat."

"But I can't read Hebrew."

"Don't worry—God is multilingual. English works pretty good."

David did just fine, and the service went on.

Everyone took turns reading from the Haggadah, which included the meaning of the Passover plate, a discussion of the years in the desert, and listing the plagues.

"Morar are bitter herbs, made out of horseradish root, to remind us of the bitterness of slavery and how servitude destroys the human spirit to this day."

Bernie smiled as the dish went around. He had grown the plant in his garden, grated the root that morning, and bottled the caustic substance. It was passed around the table, and a cacophony of wheezing, sneezing, and tears followed each bite.

"A success," cried Bernie as he noted the faces of his family. "I guess the horseradish was a success this year."

Harry continued to the next page, pointing to the charoset. "It's a sweet mix made of chopped nuts, apples, and cinnamon. It represents the mortar used to hold bricks together. Most likely used on the pyramids."

"Why is it so sweet?" asked Jack.

"Who knows?" came Harry's response. "In the Sephardic tradition, it is blended to look more like cement... in other traditions it tastes like cement."

Every item of food on the Passover plate was discussed, resulting in a debate. "Celery represents the greens of spring."

"No, it's not. It's the rebirth of man," added Alvin.

"No, that's the egg," responded Molly.

"That's bullshit," cried Sally. "Where do you get this crap? Some Reform Rabbi?"

"Okay, you're both right. Now stop it," Bernie interjected.

Finally, there was the chicken bone. Bernie pointed to it and said, "It is in place of a lamb's bone, the sacrifice originally used in the Temple each Passover."

Molly mumbled something about chicken bones being cheaper than lamb bones. "No wonder he got it," she said, pointing to her son-in-law.

Sally, overhearing her, announced in Yiddish, *"Gai kukken afen yam,"*—"Go shit in the ocean."

"Sally, what did you say?" demanded Molly.

Bernie, holding back a laugh, said, "It means a bone is on the table." He winked at his mother.

The reading of the Haggadah went on for another hour. By that time, the boys were getting drowsy. The cats and raccoon were snoring. The adults pleaded for food.

Harry noted that Easter and Passover fell about the same time of the year, both holidays commemorating the rebirth of man. The Haggadah was ended. It was time for the Seder meal.

First came the eggs, followed by gefilte fish and then chicken soup with matzo balls. The main course consisted of vegetarian chopped liver for Bernie, brisket of beef, roast chicken, veggies, potatoes, and rice and beans with mushrooms. Dessert was macaroons.

Sally, looking at her son's plate, couldn't help herself. She forked a large chunk of beef onto his plate. "Bernie, that's enough of this crap. Eat some food, for Christ's sake. You look like a bag of bones."

Bernie pushed the beef away, smiled, and dug into the rice and beans.

At the end of the Seder meal, it was time to open the door for the Prophet Elijah. Bernie couldn't contain himself. "Elijah makes the rounds to homes celebrating Passover, announcing the coming of the Messiah… but also to help sick children." He asked Mark to open the sliding doors next to the dining room so the prophet could enter.

The boy went over, pushed aside the drapes, and very slowly opened the door. The light from the full moon shone into the room.

"Elijah, have some wine," mumbled Bernie. *It's a cup just for you. Anna needs you. Are you out there? Please, please help one child.*

The night was still—not even a breeze. Bernie looked straight ahead. His eyes clouded, and tears fell down his cheeks. He let out a muffled cry. Leah came over and stroked his forehead. "It's okay, everyone. Bernie's been upset about a patient. He's fine." She whispered into his ear, "Get a grip on yourself. There's too much depending on you." He smiled.

When the Seder dinner was over, everyone helped clean up.

"Sorry to bother you, but I need some help," a strange voice called from the downstairs foyer.

Bernstein dropped the dish he was holding. Expert rolled off the couch, trotted over, and stood at Bernie's side. The two walked to the top of the stairs. They could see a man standing below.

He appeared to be middle-aged, tall, and thin with a trimmed gray beard. The man wore old hiking boots, jeans, and a flannel shirt partially covered by a leather jacket.

"I thought your driveway was the main road. Once I realized my mistake, I turned in the field, but my pickup got stuck in a snowdrift. I'd like to call for a tow truck to pull me out."

Bernie laughed. "It happens all the time—don't sweat it. Come on up while I change. I keep chains in my Jeep, and we'll get you out in no time."

Expert walked down the stairs, took a sniff of the stranger, decided he was all right, and returned to the sofa.

"Don't mind Expert. He's attack trained."

Both men laughed. Expert snarled, showed his teeth, and went back to sleep.

The man followed Bernie into the dining room and introduced himself as Al Green. He received a round of hellos. Leah offered him something to eat, but the man begged off, saying he'd been eating all night.

Bernstein threw on sweats, and the two drove in his Jeep to the pickup truck in the field. They pulled it out without incident and then shook hands. As Al left, he yelled back at Bernie, "Hey doc, maybe I can return the favor one day. Keep your chin up."

With that, he waved and drove away.

Bernstein drove back to the house, those last words echoing in his mind. *How'd he know I was a doc? Something else... What was it? "Keep your chin up"... Holy shit! CHNUP!*

He had been calling the drug CHNUP "chin up" for over a year. It was in the freezer at the office. He had completely forgotten about it.

He looked up at the bright night sky. *Of course! The drug is for adults with lung cancer. It's purely investigational. This just might be the fourth drug.*

Bernie returned to the Seder. Elijah's cup had been sipped.

Chapter 22

Days later, Bernstein called his old mentor in California.

"No! It's out of the question. You can't give CHNUP to a child. Christ's sake, it's an experimental drug."

Bernie held the receiver at arm's length. "Dave, please, you're in California. I can hear you without the phone. Stop yelling. Give me a better suggestion."

Dave Schaffer, chief of medicine at Western University Medical School, softened his voice for the moment. "Bernie, there are no other ideas. I want you to go through the reasons why you can't use the drug."

"Dave, I know why."

"Like hell you do. Why do you have CHNUP?"

"You're treating me like an intern."

"Too bad. You're acting like one. Answer the question."

He looked around his office. The lone light over his desk illuminated the snow falling outside his window. He shivered and felt it best to play the game with Schaffer. "I received the drug from the National Cancer Institute to use on adults with lung cancer who failed all treatments."

"Has it been approved by the FDA for use?"

"No, it's part of a Phase 3 study. The purpose is to get enough information to allow the drug to be used to treat lung cancer. Come on, Dave, you're the senior investigator for the program."

"Very good," Schaffer said. Bernie pictured his professor—lips tight, eyes wide open, glaring into the phone. But Schaffer wasn't finished yet. "Has it worked on anyone?"

"Dave, you know it has, but you need more numbers."

"My, my, you did your homework. However, it's only worked on adults with lung cancer."

Bernie felt the phone line tighten. Schaffer was going to come through the line. His voice tensed as he went on with the exam. "So who is eligible, and why use it if it's the same as other drugs?"

Bernstein lowered his head, spoke softly into the phone, "Look, Dave, I know it's only for lung cancer patients. That's the condition for use. On top of that, it's to be used alone." He stopped, took a deep breath.

There was a long silence broken only by the sleet pounding against the window. Bernie broke the quiet. "Dave, it might work on Anna. Its pharmacology is different from any drug she's received." He sighed. "Oh crap, I might as well tell you the full story. I'm planning on using it with three other drugs."

"You are on your own with this one. Now I've become an accomplice if I don't report you."

"Dave, that wasn't my intent in calling you. Could it work?"

"It's not for children, Hodgkin's or otherwise. You'll get sued and lose your license. I'm trying to reason with you as your friend. Use three drugs. You did your best."

"I'm not worried about the license. This kid is terminal. I've explained the side effects plus the Phase 3 study and its experimental use on lung cancer patients to Anna and her family. They're willing to go ahead. I just can't let go."

"You've always been like this." Mimicking Bernie, Schaffer said, "Dave, I've got to do what's right." Dave Schaffer resumed his regular tone. "I remember when they wanted to throw you out of the program because you treated a hemophilic with antibiotics for appendicitis. The chief of surgery told you no. I had a hell of a time keeping you on."

"Granted, it was a long shot. But that bastard refused to operate on the kid; most likely it would have ruined his surgical record." Bernie grabbed for the Spalding on his desk.

"Yes, you made your point. But you didn't have to tell him that, and besides, the kid died."

"He would have died anyway once the surgeon refused to operate. If he had allowed me to use the antibiotics earlier, it might have worked. That surgeon couldn't think his way out of a box." Bernstein's eyes began to burn, and he started to bounce the ball against the floor.

"Do you have a cold? Your voice is… rough." Dave paused and then went on. "Are you still bouncing that ball around? Jesus Christ, haven't you outgrown it yet?"

Bernie put the ball back on the desk. He wiped his eyes with tissues and blew his nose.

"Dave, I know I won't sleep nights thinking of what I might do to this kid. I'm guessing on the doses, and I've lowered them as much as I can. I can only hope it works."

"Shit! Nothing is getting through your thick head. Okay, we're getting nowhere. I know you well enough to know you'll do it anyway."

There was silence until Schaffer broke it. "Yes, your idea just might work, but, Bernie, I can't protect you. You're on your own now. By the way, what do you intend to tell the National Cancer Institute? You do have to account for the drug."

"Oh, I forgot to mention we had a power outage last month. CHNUP thawed when the electricity went out."

"I should have known you'd have the angles figured out. Well, good luck. You just might be right." The conversation ended with a click.

Bernie slowly hung up the phone and laid his head on the table. Time passed. He felt a chill, as the office thermostat had been turned down. Bernie raised his head from the desk. "Fuck it!" Then he started calculating the doses of the drugs. It was a good part guesswork with a smattering of knowledge. There were no guidelines, as he was in the realm of the unknown. He could only base everything on a guess and a gut feeling.

The snow continued to fall.

Chapter 23

During the day, he completed a plan for therapy and discussed it with the oncology nurse, Janice O'Malley.

"CHNUP? What's that?"

He told her of the planned treatment. Halfway through the explanation, she interrupted, "Bernie, I have complete faith in you, but the hospital administration won't let you get away with it."

He stared at her, mouth open. "Now what?"

"You know, if it were up to me, I'd do it. An investigational drug can't be used in this hospital. We don't have privileges for experimental drugs. We can only use those that are approved."

"So CHNUP is out?"

"Oh, stop acting so innocent. You knew damn well it wouldn't fly. Stop trying to bullshit your way through a rule you don't like."

"Shit. I better speak to the medical ethics committee."

Over the next few hours, he called the members of the committee, including his old *friend* Dr. Hampton.

"Look, Bernstein, forget about it. The answer is no. It'll never get past me. In addition, if you try using the drug anywhere, I'll make sure you lose your license. I'd be the first to throw you a drop-dead party."

"Screw you. I still want the meeting."

The committee met the next evening in a room off the main library. It was small, and a large wooden desk took up most of the space. The chairs were high-backed with soft leather seats. The entire room was dark brown with a chandelier over the middle of the desk. There were eight chairs, and Bernie sat at one end. He presented his case.

"This is an eleven-year-old girl that has been given the best treatment at Bayside University Hospital. It didn't work. She was sent back here for terminal care. I found a mistake in her diagnosis and feel that I can treat her using an investigational drug called CHNUP along with a few other drugs. I think the combination of drugs might work. Without it, she'll die."

Questions followed. "Wasn't she sent here to be made comfortable?"

"Yes, that's right, but the family and patient want treatment. I agree with them."

"Has it been tried before?"

"No."

"Why do you think it'll work?"

"It's logical. Besides, it's her last chance."

Hampton leaped out of his seat. "You are one arrogant fool. If you think that I'll allow my hospital to be used for experimentation, then you are dumber than I thought. You make me sick looking at you. What makes you smarter than the professors at the university?"

"I didn't say I'm smarter, Hampton, and in case you haven't noticed, this is not your hospital. I'm simply saying that I'm trying to save an eleven-year-old child." Bernie bit his tongue and squeezed the Spalding in his pocket. "What I propose just might work. I'm going to do it whether you like it or not."

Hampton had had enough. "You can stop right now. I will not allow any further discussion of this subject. Bernstein does whatever he wants. Rules, regulations mean nothing to him. The safety of the child means nothing, neither does the dignity of the hospital." By this time, Hampton's face was scarlet. With his finger pointing at Bernstein, he said, "I will report you and this hospital to the licensing board if you try it. If that occurs, Bernstein, you will lose your license and the hospital its accreditation." Hampton slammed his fist on the table.

The committee voted the idea down. That ended the meeting. A few members came up to Bernie afterward, giving sympathetic pats on his back. Their hands were tied. Hampton walked out without a word.

Bernie sat in his chair for a long time, fists clenched, tears flowing down his cheeks. He got up slowly, walked to the nurses' station on Anna's floor, and picked up her chart. There was only one course of action—discharge her in the morning and treat her at home.

Fuck 'em.

He went directly to Anna's room. Bella was rubbing Anna's forehead, and she was watching a television program about birds. Jessica was in another room caring for a patient. Bernie fetched her, and all four sat in the room on the bed or in chairs. Bernie couldn't sit still and got up to pace the room. The pink ball moved from one hand to the other. "We have to change plans. Because one of the drugs is experimental, we can't administer it in this hospital."

Bella looked at him. "What kind of crap is this? Anna's been tormented by everyone, and now that we have this chance, they won't let her be treated?"

"Bella, hold tight, let me finish. We can treat her at home. It's risky, but I can give her the drugs, and if for any reason she has to be readmitted, we'll do so."

"Bernie, are you suggesting she'll get the same medicines at home as here?"

"Absolutely. I have access to all the drugs necessary, including the experimental one. There isn't any reason it can't be given outside the hospital."

Jessica smiled, and soon Anna and Bella were smiling too.

Bernie nodded. "You'll have to keep the house as clean as possible. She'll be exposed to all kinds of bugs, but it's probably no worse than staying in the hospital. You'll have to wear face masks and gloves and dress as if you're in an operating room, but it will work." He stopped pacing and then started up again. "I'll make the arrangements, but damn it, we can do it." He sighed. "Once she's treated, we can always bring her back to the hospital for critical care and high-dose antibiotics. Home care may be only for the chemo."

The following morning, Anna left the hospital in an ambulance. Freshly laundered operating gowns, booties, and gloves went along. Bernstein gave a weak smile and waved.

His final instructions: "I'll stop by this evening. Call me if there are any problems. Anna, try to drink the liquid meals that I prescribed and eat plenty of ice cream."

Chapter 24

He went to Anna's home at the end of office hours. On the way over, the sun was shining, the snow had started melting, and spring was in the air.

When he arrived, Earl the Doberman greeted him with a snarl and clamped down on his pants leg, holding tight.

"Nice doggie—die."

Bernstein walked the rest of the way dragging his left leg with the rotten dog attached.

Once he was on the porch, Bella greeted him. "Hi Bernie," she said. "Bad Earl. You're a naughty dog." She gave him a treat. Earl wolfed it down and gave her a smile.

So much for dog training.

Glass enclosed the porch. Anna lay in a bed, knees folded into her chest. Pieces of broken hair lay over the pillow. On the right side of the bed was a white wicker table. On top sat a wide rectangular reading lamp with a flowered shade. There was a large glass of water full of ice cubes and lemon slices. A small vase contained yellow daffodils surrounded by wood ferns.

Jessica sat behind her, softly cooing while stroking Anna's shoulders. Bella pulled over a chair for Bernstein and then found one for herself.

He sat down, smiling at the women.

"Bernie, would you like some coffee?"

He nodded, as did Bella. Jessica went off to the kitchen. Bernstein asked about Anna's comfort.

"Yes, cramps in my stomach... All the time... No, I didn't move my bowels... No, I can't eat. Food makes the cramps worse... Yes, I can drink soup, ginger ale, apple juice."

It went on and on. Anna started to cry. Bella held her. Bernstein stopped asking.

Jessica brought in the coffee, steaming hot with milk, cream, sugar, and a side plate of pastries. They sat in silence for a time.

"Anna, you're going to get better. I know it."

For the first time, he didn't cross his fingers.

Anna stopped crying and put her arms out, and he leaned toward her. She gave him a kiss.

He smiled. "Let's talk about the drugs that I think will work." Bernie explained in detail the drugs he'd use including the investigational nature of CHNUP. "You must understand that the drug has not been released for general use. I happen to have it only under special conditions that I use it on adults with lung cancer when all other treatments have failed." He went on to explain how the drug worked.

"I believe it's the missing drug that I've been looking for."

Anna stopped paying attention. Bella and Jessica heard but didn't listen. They wanted to get started.

Bernstein looked at Anna and gently stroked her arm. Once he caught her attention, he explained the drug again. She got the message and nodded agreement.

Again, Bella asked when he'd start.

"Tomorrow, if you all understand what's involved."

Jessica lowered her head and then looked up at Bernstein. "You're taking a big risk. You could lose your license. I know you're aware that may happen, but we want you to treat her. We'll take full responsibility."

"That's kind of you, but it doesn't work that way. It's my problem."

"No, Bernie, we can't let you do this." It was Bella's turn. "We'll make sure that nothing is said about this drug. No one is allowed in the house as long as Anna's sick. We can all promise you that it'll end here, and when it works…" she smiled.

Bernie said, "Frankly, I haven't thought about consequences. I'm suggesting this as the only treatment. I've discussed my plan with experts in the field. They all think I'm nuts but have no other ideas. I don't regret using these medicines as long as I feel it's best for Anna."

The room was quiet. Bella spoke. "Bernie, do what you think will work."

The women nodded.

Shit, does anyone listen?

"I feel this is the best approach, but we're dealing with possible fatal doses. The combination could result in Anna's death."

It was as though a vacuum had sucked up the voices. Silence.

A yellow-breasted bird flew onto the windowsill and started chirping, breaking the quiet. They all looked at the bird.

Finally, Jessica was the first to speak. "Bernie, go over the drugs again," she had tears in her eyes as she spoke.

He repeated the plan in full detail, emphasizing the experimental nature of the drug, and finished by saying, "It's against the law to use in Anna's case. I know that I've repeated myself a number of times, but I want you all to understand the devastating problem that we're up against. If nothing else, it's for my sake that I keep repeating." Then he gave his reasons. "I'll combine CHNUP with three other drugs, one in very high doses called Methotrexate. The last drug has to be neutralized by another injectable drug called leucovorum, which must be given about twenty-four hours after the Methotrexate."

He stopped speaking and looked at the bird, who was now staring at him.

That bird is listening. The bird nodded. *Christ, what now?*

"Jessica, I'll leave the leucovorum in your refrigerator. If for any reason I can't get back, you'll have to give the shot."

Jessica shook her head. "Bernie, don't ask me to treat my granddaughter. I can't do it."

He started to protest but then stopped. *Ah—screw it.* "Look, Jessica, I'll show you anyway. No need to worry; I'll be here."

Quiet descended over the room. They looked at the bird. Bernie took a deep breath, Bella's eyes widened, and Jessica started crying. In sequence, Anna, Bella, Jessica, and finally the bird gave their nods.

"Good. I'll bring the drugs tomorrow and give Anna the first shots." He took a deep breath. "Then I'll be back on Wednesday for the rescue drug." He thought for a few seconds. "Ordinarily, you'd have to sign a consent form, but we're breaking so many rules it's not worth the ink."

He headed home. As he started the car, he opened the windows and could feel a cool breeze. His headlights caught buds on the trees. The night smiled. Bernstein's chest swelled. "Damn, I feel good!"

Chapter 25

Bernie ended office hours early the following day and went directly to Anna's home. As he walked to the porch, Earl latched onto his pant leg. Again he dragged the dog into the house. Anna lay on the same bed in the closed-in porch with Jessica and Bella on each side. Bella called Earl a bad dog and gave him the snack. Earl smiled; Bernie growled.

He declined the offered cup of coffee. It would have been the eighth of the day.

"Let's go over the treatment again." He did. All three nodded. They understood... maybe.

Bernstein took the medications from his black leather case and laid each on the table beside the bed. They included a pouch of sodium chloride solution attached to a plastic tube, CHNUP, and Methotrexate. His hand went into the case again and extracted two bottles of pills, which he tossed on the bed.

Anna closed her eyes. "Is it going to hurt?"

"A small pinch. You may get sick to your stomach in the morning. That's normal. It means the drug is working."

Bella and Jessica held hands.

Bernstein placed a tourniquet around her thin arm. The veins had been severely damaged by previous IVs. He picked the Spalding ball out of his pocket. "Come on, kid, give it a squeeze," he said, and she did with great effort.

He kept at her. She continued. Finally, a small vein popped up. Bernie washed the skin with alcohol and placed a small needle with a short tube into the vein. Blood appeared immediately.

He quickly attached the tubing to the bag of liquid and opened the pressure valve of the bag. The fluid flowed into Anna's vein. "We're done," he muttered. He looked at Anna. Her eyes were closed.

"Did it hurt?"

"Not yet."

"Now for the first drug." He injected the Methotrexate through a small port on the tubing and noted the time: 6:00 p.m. "Jessica, remember, if for some reason I'm not back by six tomorrow evening, you have to give the leucovorum."

She turned her back to him, held her hands to her face, and walked away.

Bernstein sighed, took out the CHNUP, and injected the drug into the bag. He slowed down the drip of sodium chloride. Anna didn't show any change in expression. They waited, holding their breath. Anna lay back. Her eyes closed, and she went to sleep.

It took time for the bag containing the investigational drug to empty. He then extracted the needle.

Anna opened her eyes. "That didn't hurt."

"Sorry to disappoint you."

"Is it really over?"

"Yep."

"Wow. That must have been some course you took at correspondence school."

"I gave them special-delivery envelopes, so I was first to get my grades. I guess you could consider me top of the class." He stopped smiling and went on with more instructions, explaining in detail about the two bottles of pills he had removed from his bag.

"Here they are. Make sure you finish both." Bernstein got up, walked to the refrigerator, and placed the rescue drug inside with a needle and syringe. He reminded Jessica again about the leucovorum. There was no reply.

On the way home, it was another clear night, no clouds, owls hooting, and waves lapping against the rocks on the shores of the inlets. He arrived to the usual commotion. Sally was busy running around, giving one boy after another big wet kisses. Molly kept shaking her head. She looked up, saw Bernstein enter the room, and went back to reading the *New York Times* Art Review. Alvin sat quietly next to her reading *Architectural Review*.

Bernie overheard Molly telling him that Leah should have married that lawyer from Yale. Alvin smirked. Bernstein shrugged. He'd heard it all before.

Harry was drinking scotch with no cubes but a splash of water to keep Sally quiet. The *Wall Street Journal* lay on his lap. As soon as he saw his son enter, Harry smiled and said, "Those goddamn Democrats are gonna ruin the county."

Bernie walked over, gave his father a kiss on his bald head, and said, "So Nixon is all of a sudden a bargain?" They both smiled at this friendly disagreement, which had gone on for years.

Russell was busy making supper in his usual kitchen outfit—white jockey shorts, T-shirt, and apron. He was dancing to music from a small radio off to the side. Bernie gave him a pat on the behind as he walked by. Russell giggled.

Leah came over and gave him a big kiss. "Bernie, you better not have any plans for tomorrow."

He looked at her, puzzled. "Well, President Ford wanted me to fly down to Washington. Seems he needs some help."

"You better tell him another day. They're expecting snow, and my knee is killing me." Ever since Leah broke her kneecap tripping over a litter of puppies, the knee was the best indicator of storms. She went on. "This is going to be a big one."

"Oh, come on. It's a beautiful night. So we have a few sprinkles. Nope, spring is here, and my garden is going in soon."

"You should try listening to the weather forecast, but I know it's not your nature."

"They're always wrong. Besides, they called for snow. No storm, no gloom. It'll be a great day."

The supper was delicious and full of calories—pasta with Russell's special fresh lemon-and-cream sauce covered with large chunks of New England lobster and clams. Gobs of garlic-butter bread sat on the table to dunk in the sauce.

Russell glowed with pride. Bernie complained about his arteries but took seconds.

After dinner Sally, Leah, and Russell cleaned up the kitchen. Bernie picked up a medical journal. Harry told the boys stories about his childhood in Russia living in a ghetto under the czar. Molly told stories of her grandfather living on the czar's estate.

Bernstein mumbled to the boys that he had probably shoveled shit.

It was getting late, homework was finished, and the adults were getting sleepy. Bernstein slept the sleep of the innocent.

Chapter 26

Coastal New England awoke to a whiteout.

So much for sprinkles.

"Stay off the roads! Hazards everywhere," blared a voice on the radio, which suddenly went dead. Bernstein grabbed a phone. No tone. "Damn, the lines are down. I can't call Jessica." He looked at his watch—8:00 a.m. He had ten hours to give Anna the leucovorum. Bernstein dressed quickly, threw a shovel in the Jeep, and started down the driveway. He stopped. The snow was already a foot deep, not counting drifts.

He returned to the house; tossed his cross-country skis, poles, gloves, and boots in with the shovel; donned a ski mask; and headed into the storm.

The roads were buried, and he soon found himself stuck in a large snowbank. Shoveling didn't help, and Bernstein was fifteen miles from Anna.

The snow was much too deep to ski, so he trudged toward the police station. The wind had created walls of snow, but he was able to push forward.

How stupid can I be? No snow. Flurries only. Stop it, Bernstein. You'll make it. Get going.

Eventually, a partially plowed road allowed him to put on his skis and travel slowly to the station. His face was on fire from the wind and cold. The goggles kept the snow from his eyes.

Bernie arrived at the station, took off his skis, placed them on his shoulder, and walked into the office. The room was a mess. There were coffee cups strewn about, floors wet from the melting snow, and overcoats tossed in piles on chairs. Cops were everywhere, speaking on walkie-talkies to whomever.

"Sir, we're trying to get through. We only have a few snowmobiles."

"Yes, lady, we're in touch with the fire station."

"EMS is on the way."

"I know your husband is sick; we're trying to get there."

"Look, lady, this is the fourth time you've called. I told you before we can't help your cat."

The desk sergeant screamed out, "Where did everyone get so many fuckin' ham radios?" He stopped and looked at the doctor. "Get those skis out of here. What the hell do you want?"

"Sergeant, I have to see a patient in—"

"Hey guys, stop what you're doing. The doc needs a favor. He has to see a patient." Sarcasm oozed from his mouth.

"Let me finish, for Christ's sake. This is an eleven-year-old girl, and she needs medicine today." He tried to explain the problem but didn't get far. Cop voices from all parts of the room drowned Bernie out.

"Charlie, call off the storm. The doc's got to see a patient."

"Hey doc, if we call it off, can we charge Blue Cross?"

"I bet you get big bucks for a house call. Must be a rich patient. I'd charge double."

"Quiet! I gave this kid a big drug yesterday, and she needs another drug today. She lives in Seaside, and I have to get there before five o'clock."

"Doc, you should have thought about that yesterday. Things ain't moving today." He stopped, took a deep breath. "What the fuck is wrong with you? Can't you see we have problems?"

"Thank you, dear," he muttered.

"Doc, I just told you—traffic ain't moving today and we can't spare anyone. Come to think of it, you just might stand on the corner and wait for a bus." That drew a laugh from the cops.

"Hey doc, here's a quarter for the bus. Good luck." More snickering from the group.

"I'm not taking your bullshit. I'm getting there. Didn't anyone come in on a snowmobile?"

Joe Clark walked over. "Doc, I came in on my snowmobile. I can take you to the station in Crestwood. That's on the way and might help."

He shook Joe's hand, remembering a year earlier when Clark's wife had been diagnosed with an inoperable cancer. The family wanted her to see an oncologist, which was how she came to see Bernstein. It had turned out that she didn't have cancer but rather a benign cyst on the liver. Bernie had reassured the family that all was well and then gave the referring doctor hell for scaring the family.

The sergeant yelled that Clark couldn't take a civilian on his snowmobile during work hours.

Joe Clark walked to the sergeant's desk. "Can it. It's my snowmobile, and I'm going home for a few hours. Stop breaking his chops. Besides, he's done me plenty of favors."

The sergeant continued to grumble, but Bernie was off with Joe Clark. "Don't mind him, doc. He's been up all night, and since we can't do much, he's frustrated. He's really a good guy."

They arrived at the station in Crestwood. Before Joe went home, they shook hands again.

The police at the Crestwood station had set up snowmobile runs to the surrounding towns. They had the situation in better control, and once he explained the problem, they were able to give him a ride to just a few miles from Anna's home. He skied the rest of the way over partially plowed roads.

Anna was in a central bedroom. Bella had set up a cot next to her bed. Bernie came in as she was trying to feed her daughter. There was a small propane heater nearby upon which sat a pot of soup and a pot of coffee. The electricity was off, but Anna seemed comfortable in a quilt, hat, and gloves. Bella and Jessica were also wrapped in coats: Bella in fur to her ankles and Jessica in a heavy woolen coat with a sweatshirt underneath. A large fire burned full blast in a wood stove nearby, giving off enough heat for comfort. Bernie took off his coat.

"Hey, kid, how's it going?"

"I feel sick, like I want to puke. Did you give me the right stuff? I got a lot sicker at Bayside."

"That's because I used a magic elixir."

Christ, I hope I gave her enough.

She gave him a smile. Jessica brought out the leucovorum in a syringe with the needle attached. He was on time.

"Okay, here's the shot."

"Yikes, that hurt."

"Sorry, it's over for the moment."

Everyone relaxed, including Earl, who for whatever reason decided not to bite. Bernie had coffee, as did the women. They chatted for a half hour or more. The snow slowed, and the wind came up. The phones were still down. He couldn't call home or the hospital.

"Well, I better get going."

"Bernie, stay here tonight. We have plenty of room."

"Thanks, Bella, but I've got to see what's going on at the hospital. I have a feeling that very few doctors showed up, and there are still patients there that have to be seen."

"How do you plan on getting there?"

"I assume they've plowed more roads by this time, and I can ski the rest of the way." He explained the plans for the next few weeks. "I'll have someone from the laboratory stop by every few days to draw blood from Anna. Once I get the report, I'll give you a call."

He pulled at his left ear and then went on. "I'll stop by daily to see Anna on my way home from the office. Just keep her away from people." He stopped, looked at Earl. "And dogs."

Earl looked at him and ever so slowly walked out of the room.

Bernstein started to put his coat back on and then added, "I'll stop by the fire station on my way to the hospital and ask if they can stop by the house periodically just in case there's trouble. I'm sure they'll agree." He left into grayness, thinking of the next few weeks.

Shit, I hope I didn't give her too much of the drugs. "The worst will come when her blood count drops," he mumbled to no one.

Suppose the concoction doesn't work.

Damn it! It will work. Stop being negative.

He did have to ski the few miles, but it made him relax. The air was fresh, and the vigor of skiing loosened his brain. Along the way, he stopped at the firehouse. The chief assured him that it wouldn't be a problem to check in on the family periodically. He'd known them for years and was glad to help.

Bernie finally arrived at the hospital. It was seven in the evening; Belmira Almeida, the nursing supervisor for the night shift, greeted him. "Dr. Bernstein, am I glad to see you. The nurses have been working two shifts, and they're beat. We can't get in touch with any of the staff doctors."

"Didn't anyone come in?"

"No, you're the only one, and the phones are down."

"I know. I couldn't call. Okay, let's get to work. Are there a lot of patients?"

"Enough. Are you going to see them all?"

"Belmira, got any other ideas? Sounds like I'm the only game in town."

He stopped, blew his nose, and went on. "We just have to warn the patients that I'm covering for their doctor. They all don't have cancer. Last time one lady passed out. She thought I was the *angel of death* making hospital rounds."

It went well. No one fainted, and most were glad to see him.

When he finally bedded down for the night, sleep wouldn't come. Thoughts of Anna controlled his brain. Finally he let go, thinking, *Screw you, Bernstein. Stop worrying. It won't do any good. You did what you could.*

Bernie then thought of Leah and had to speak to her. At that moment the hospital intercom notified him to call his home. Leah answered on the first ring. Bernie couldn't contain himself. "Are you all right? Do you have enough heat?"

"Yes, we're fine. I was so worried about you. Did Anna get her shot?"

"Anna got her shot, and I've made rounds at the hospital."

"My God, Bernie, I've been sitting by the phone since you left. Are you sure you're safe?" Before he could answer, she was talking again. "Bernie, if you do this again, I'm going with you. I can't stand the waiting. There is no way you're going out there without me."

Leah quieted down. Bernie assured her that he was fine; he missed her.

"Well, next time listen to the weather forecast."

"Babe, I don't have to—I have you. Besides, they were wrong. They predicted light snow."

"Oh, shut up and go to sleep… I love you."

Bernstein smiled, sent his love back, and went to sleep.

Chapter 27

The following day, the city was still covered in snow. The phone lines were up, but travel wasn't. Bernie made rounds, seeing the patients and chatting with each.

"Hi, Mr. Warren. How're ya doin'?"

Warren pulled at his bathrobe rope to tighten it. He was a large-boned man with a reddish face. "Doc, I'm feeling a lot better. Think I can go home soon?"

"I spoke to Dr. Graham this morning. He wants you to stay in for a stress test. He thinks the cold weather could affect your heart. I'm afraid you'll be here for a few more days."

Warren frowned and lay back in the bed. So it went throughout most of the day. Fortunately, there weren't any major problems.

He called home. Leah answered the phone. "Don't worry—we're fine." Small talk continued. "Oh, Harry wants to drive home. He claims he has a pinochle game tonight in New Jersey."

Bernie laughed. "That old battle axe thinks he's back in Russia. The snow doesn't bother him. Eighty years old and ready to go to a card game, even if it's four hundred miles away."

"Not to worry—Russell hid his keys. Then he and Alvin challenged him to a game tonight. That made Harry happy."

He called Anna's home. Bella answered. "She's nauseated and won't eat much. I did get some soup and ice cream into her."

"That's good. Keep it up. I'm at the hospital until they plow the roads. It should be a few days at most. Let me know if there are any changes in her condition."

He needed exercise and started walking and then running around the corridors. "Out of the way. Doctor Decathlon." One of the nurses slapped a number on his back.

He soon tired of the track meet, bundled up, and went outside to the parking lot. He packed some snow and started throwing snowballs at one of the hospital walls. It didn't take long before he felt a whack on his back. He turned; two nurses were behind him tossing snowballs at him.

"Fight, fight!" And so it went. Bernie had no chance as more hospital personnel joined the fray. Patients lined the windows, cheering. Bernstein started laughing and was soon joined by the others.

The sun started to set, yet the fight went on. The sky turned from blue to gray and then black. Snow began to fall.

I've got to see Anna tomorrow.

The game ended. He and a few nurses went to the hospital cafeteria, where they ate supper and told stories. Bernie picked at his plate, ate half, excused himself, and left to find an empty room. Before crashing for the night, he called home. All was well.

Bernie buried himself under the covers and tried to get some sleep. The noise from the plows kept him awake most of the night.

The morning was clear. Frost clouded his window. He ventured outside in his hospital scrub suit, took a deep breath, coughed twice, and decided that it was colder than the day before. The streets were clear. Bernstein gave a thumbs-up to the Department of Snow Plowing. No one noticed.

He called home. Leah answered. "Bernie, we're all fine. The boys and Russell shoveled the driveway last night. It's passable."

"Really? All four hundred feet? I can't believe it."

"Russell and I are coming to get you. We found your Jeep in a snowbank, and the boys dug it out. We'll be at the hospital in about an hour. I'll drive the wagon, and Russell will drive the Jeep."

"That's great. I can't come right home. I have to see Anna, and I promised to stop by to see a few other patients."

Chapter 28

The doctors' parking lot was filling up just as Leah arrived, followed by Russell. The three went into the cafeteria for coffee.

"Bernie, hospitals get me so nervous. Look at these people. They have dreadful diseases, and I'm going to catch something horrible. Leah, please take me home. I want to die in my own bed." He raised his arms, covering his eyes.

Bernstein kept a straight face, nodding. "I'm afraid you're right, Russell. That man right behind you has tuberculosis, and I noticed that he coughed on your shoulder."

Russell jumped straight up, turned around, and looked at an empty chair. "Very funny, Bernie."

Leah reported that the kids and grandparents were fine, especially since they had learned that school was canceled for the rest of the week due to the snow. This gave the grandparents more time to spend with the boys.

They finished their coffee. Bernie gave both a hug. The two cars drove off in separate directions: Russell and Leah heading for home, Bernie to Anna's house.

The roads had packed snow and ice. On either side, there were eight-foot snowdrifts. He drove slower than usual. When he arrived, instead of knocking, he walked right in. The heat felt good. Anna was in the living room sitting on an overstuffed couch. A blanket covered her from head to toe. Only her eyes were visible. He walked over to her to say hello. Before he could say anything, Anna started to cry.

"Bernie, I'm so sick. Please… get me… better."

Bella walked into the room. Showing little surprise that Bernie was there, she gave him a weak smile and sat on the couch next to her daughter, softly holding her hand.

Bernie nodded to Bella and then looked at his patient. "Anna, I know you'll get better."

Jessica came down the stairs. "Bernie, I didn't hear you come in. Did Earl bother you?"

"No. I'm glad you have him sitting on the enclosed porch and not near Anna. But I get the feeling that he likes me." At that moment, Bernie had an impulse to walk over to Earl in the other room, which he did and gave him a few pats. "Earl, you're a good guy and very understanding." That got him a smile and then a lick. He then left the room, washed his hands, and went back to see Anna. While pulling up a chair, he said "Bring me up to date."

She had the same problems but worse: cramps, constipation, lack of appetite. Her exam remained unchanged.

"It's too early to expect any real problems or changes from the chemotherapy. Anna will get sores in her mouth in a few days, and I'm afraid she'll lose her hair, but it will all come back."

"Bernie, when will she feel better?" It was Jessica's turn.

He looked at the three women. "Anna's going to get better—I hope within a month." He stopped, looked at his shoes, and went on. "We have to make changes as of now. You have all the hospital gowns, scrub suits, gloves, facemasks, and hats. Whoever comes into Anna's room has to wear those hospital greens, put on the facemask, and wash every time. You can't wash enough. In addition, no one is allowed in the house other than the four of us."

He turned, looked at Earl, and in a voice loud enough for the dog to hear said, "I'm afraid, old buddy, you'll have to stay in that room until Anna's blood work comes back to normal." Earl looked at him and slowly got up, tail between his legs. His ears drooped, and he sulked to the outermost corner of the porch.

Bernie watched the dog walk away. Anna demanded to know more about these new rules. "But, Dr. Bernie, you brought Earl into the hospital!"

"Anna, your blood count is going to fall to very low levels, at which point there is a possibility of infections and bleeding. We all carry germs. Animals are the biggest offenders. You will have to be in isolation until your counts come up. I can't take any chances."

Bella spoke up. "A friend of ours will gladly kennel Earl and take care of him until Anna is well again. It won't be a problem."

They all looked at Anna. She didn't protest too much. Bernie put on his coat and left.

He decided to make a few more stops before going home. First was Joe Ferreira. Their walkway was full of snow. Bernstein grabbed the shovel that he carried in the back of the Jeep, took a deep breath, and went to work. In twenty minutes, the stairs were conquered. Bernie didn't bother ringing the bell but instead opened the door to the house. "I'm coming up the stairs. Everyone get your clothes on."

"Hey doc, what's a nice Jewish boy like you doing out in a night like this?"

"I was told I had a sausage deficiency, so here I am."

Susan smiled. "Well, you just sit yourself down, and I'll cook it right up."

"Thanks, Susan, but I can't do it, especially tonight. I have more calls to make."

Joe was sitting in his wheelchair, but Bernie was able to do a cursory exam. His patient was stable. "Okay, buddy, you're the same. Anything I can do?"

"You're doing plenty. Doc, I'm not quitting until the Sox win the World Series."

Bernie blinked. He smiled. "In that case, you'll outlive all of us."

That brought a laugh.

Susan took a deep breath. "In spite of Joe's paralysis, I still have my husband with me. As you've said, the cancer has stopped growing." She took a mouthful of beer and went on. "His cancer has been stable for close to six months now. Is that common?"

Bernie pulled on his ear. "Cancer is strange. It slows down in some patients, especially cancer of the prostate. Why? The stars line up in the right order. I have no idea."

Susan ordered him to stay put. She'd be back shortly with his favorite Portugese vegetable sandwich, chioriza. "You can eat it in the car."

He waited, sat down, and chatted with Joe. Due to the icy conditions, Bernie decided to eat in the house. Joe smiled and ordered food for the three of them. "Coming up," yelled Susan.

While eating, the conversation centered on the stability of Joe's cancer. Bernie, munching away, couldn't explain the whys. "All I know is that these events happen." Then, looking at Joe, he said, "I think the answer is within you. What makes you different?"

"I don't know, doc. You know that the paralysis came on quickly. I was working construction at the time, so I felt strong. That may have something to do with it."

Susan shook her head. "We've been sweethearts since the sixth grade. That's over forty years, and I know him better than anyone else. He's just not a quitter." She wiped away tears. "I think that's the answer, along with his incredible strength."

"Susan is right. Don't give up as long as your life is worth living." Bernie looked around the room; he pointed to models of planes and boats. "That hobby of yours helps. Your models have become more and more complex. That kind of work keeps people going."

The other two nodded. "I feel people pick the time to die." He stopped. "Joe, you just ain't ready and won't be for a long time."

They had finished the food. Bernstein put on his coat and was about to leave when a thought occurred. "You sure ain't going to be ready to leave this planet if it depends on the Sox winning."

He could hear both of them laughing as he closed the door.

The next stop was at the home of an old patient of his with a chronic lung condition who had spiked a fever earlier in the day. Bernie walked in, said the usual hellos, and walked over to his patient, Manny Costa. After a few cursory questions, he checked the oxygen flow from the tank and then listened to Manny's chest.

"Iris, it wouldn't hurt if you stopped buying Manny cigarettes."

"Dr. Bernie, he makes such a fuss that I can't stand it. I finally gave up. You tell him."

Before Bernie could say anything, Manny started protesting. "Doc, it's the only vice left for me. Give me another idea."

"Okay, you have a young grandson going to college. He called me a month ago asking about your condition. Remember? I told you I spoke to him."

He remembered.

"Good, tell him you need a few joints."

"Dr. Bernstein, are you suggesting that I have him get me *pot?*"

"There are enough articles that mention the benefits of cannabis. It seems it increases the appetite, relieves discomfort, and will cut down on cigarette consumption."

"How will that happen?"

"You won't be able to afford cigarettes."

Bernstein passed the news to Iris. As he was leaving, he heard her calling her grandson.

"Stephen, guess what the doctor told us to get for Grandpa…"

He quietly closed the door behind him.

He arrived home late. Everyone was asleep except for Leah. She had supper ready, lentil soup with a rice and beans dish along with veggies. He loved her with his eyes; she air-kissed him back. Bernstein poked at the food, brought a spoonful of soup to his lips, sipped, and let it drop back into the bowl. He was motionless for a short time, looking at the plate. Finally, he started picking at the rice.

Leah sat across the table, staring at her salmon. She too nursed the food. Neither spoke. They cleaned the hardly eaten meal without a word, went up to the bedroom, got into bed, and drew up the covers. He lay there with his arm under her neck. Time passed.

"Bernie, talk to me. Why are you doing this?"

At first, he didn't answer. "I don't know. I've seen too many people die from cancer when there isn't any hope. Now here's a kid who just might have a chance. I can't quit."

"The other doctors have given up. You told me so."

"Yes, they did, but they were treating the wrong disease. Those guys used drugs for lymphoma, which are similar to those used in Hodgkin's but not quite the same. That's where I see a possibility. On top of that, no one thought of CHNUP." He drew his hands from under the covers, pulled on his ear, and went on. "Anna is still alive and has enough energy to keep fighting. Since that's the case, I can't give up."

He fell silent. She looked at him. "What is driving you?"

Bernie stared at the ceiling. "I can't really describe it. I feel I'm being pulled in the right direction and can't turn back."

Leah sat up in bed. "Are you, of all people, talking about divine intervention?"

"No... yes. I don't know. I have a sense that there's more in the universe, let's say a powerful entity, albeit one in which there is both order and chaos. At times I find some logic among the chaos; a door opens, and I'm amazed." Bernie stopped, looked at his wife, kissed her forehead, and held her tightly into himself. "Anna has given me this chance. It's a small one, but she just might live. How did it happen? Where did the ideas come from? On top of all that, why me? Believe me, I'm scared shitless that I'll make a mistake and hurt her."

Leah lay back in bed. Bernie turned to his wife. "Most of the time oncology treatments are not understandable, and we fight the unknown."

He kissed her mouth, neck, and ears. They fell asleep in each other's arms.

The next morning Bernstein arose early. The boys were still out of school and sitting around the table enjoying Russell's pancakes. Sally and Harry were getting ready to leave later in the day. Leah had arranged for a taxi to take them to the airport for their flight home. They had friends at the other end to carry them the rest of the way.

Allan spoke quietly to Russell. "Don't forget we're sledding down the hill today. You've got to drive the car."

Bernstein looked at Allan and then David and finally Russell. "What hill? There's no hill around here," said Russell. He looked completely confused.

"Oh shit. No, no. Russell, don't listen to them. No hills. Last time I almost broke my neck," screamed Bernstein.

"Would all of you stop this very moment?" Russell had climbed onto a kitchen chair, hands on his hips. "I will not have a commotion in my kitchen so early in the morning. What are you lunatics talking about?"

"Ice—the dreaded ice hill. These rotten kids will talk you into driving one of the cars up and down the driveway in front of the house until it turns to ice. I'll have to park at the base and then try walking up the face of the ice cliff. Meanwhile, they'll be able to sled four hundred yards down the driveway." He turned to face Russell directly. "Last time, I kept falling all the way up to the house. I had to finish on my ass."

Leah came up from behind. She ran her hand through his hair. "Honey, do you have to go in today? Why not stay home? We would love it."

"Nah, I've got to go in."

"You've been on call for over a week. Stay home unless there's an emergency. Don't you think they can get along without you for a day?"

He thought about it, shrugged his shoulders. "All right, I have to check with Maria to see how the schedule is set for the day. If that's not a problem, I still have to see Anna, but I can do that later."

After wishing their parents good-bye and breathing a long sigh of relief, Bernie called his office. His patients would be rescheduled.

"Okay, boys, you get the cardboard. I'll get the car." The family spent the rest of the day sliding down the driveway.

Later that day, Bernie called on Anna. There wasn't much change. He decided to stop by the Whitestones' home. Marge was sleeping. Jo was crying in the kitchen, and George was patting her on the back. "Jo, Mama is comfortable. You've been a big help to both of us. I guess it's time to let nature take over."

She turned toward her father, held his hands to her mouth, and kissed them. "Papa, I know you're right. I just feel so helpless." George nodded and held his daughter closer. Bernie walked over.

"Dr. Bernstein, we didn't hear you come in. Can I get you something to drink?"

"No, Jo. Didn't mean to startle you both. I did knock. When there wasn't an answer, I just walked in. How's Marge doing?"

George walked over to him, started to shake the doctor's hand, stopped, and hugged him.

This time Bernie didn't move away. The two men held onto to each other. There wasn't much to do, so they stood around talking about nothing. Before saying good-bye, he handed George new prescriptions. Then he walked out into the cold night air and sat in the car for a good ten minutes. Finally, he turned the ignition on and started slowly toward home.

Chapter 29

The following day, the sun glistened off the frozen snow. The driveway was a sheet of ice from the previous day's sledding. Bernstein carefully made his way to his car. In spite of his care, he still fell on his ass three times. The drive to work was just as torturous.

"Maria, you're fired. I want you out of here in an hour."

"Good, I don't want to work here anyway." She stood up, grabbed her coat and handbag, and headed for the door.

A moment later, Bernie's head popped out of his office. "Maria, call the lab. I want the results of Anna's blood work as soon as possible." He watched her putting on her coat. "What the hell are you doing? Take off your coat. You're not walking to the lab."

"I'm not doing your work. I'm going home. You fired me, remember?"

"Oh… I forgot. Well, I'll give you a trial period. Now get the lab work." He disappeared back into his office.

A new patient stood in front of Maria's window trying to make an appointment.

"Maria, I thought the doctor was a nice man. He sounds awful."

Maria laughed. "He fires me when he's in a bad mood. Must have been a rough ride in today. I've been fired seven times already. Usually I ignore him, but this time I felt like giving it back."

"He seems awful," mumbled the patient.

"No, he's very considerate—the best boss I've had. He's nervous right now. Whenever he fired me in the past, he quickly apologized and gave me a raise."

Bernstein heard part of this conversation as he went back to his office. Once inside, he sat at his desk, picked up the Spalding, and threw it against the wall.

Shit, now I have to chase the ball.

Bernie started his office hours, which went on for most of the morning without any information about Anna. Bernstein checked his watch every fifteen minutes.

"Maria, any news yet?"

"Maria, call the goddamn lab. Tell them to get off their asses." Finally, the intercom rang. All he heard were squeaks and gibberish. Bernstein ran into the hall. The laboratory work was back.

It was two days after Bernie had seen Anna and seven days after she had the chemotherapy.

The shit should hit the fan today. Therapy has had a week to work.

He called Anna's home. "Jessica, Anna's blood work came in. Her white blood count is low at two thousand. Normal is five thousand. In addition, both her platelets and red blood count have fallen. It's the chemo. How's she doing?"

"No real change. Her mouth is a little sore, but I don't see any problems. She's eating a bit more, but that's about it."

"Check her temperature twice a day. If it goes up even two degrees, call me. No aspirin—Tylenol only. I'll stop by tonight."

"Suppose we can't get hold of you?"

"Take her right to the hospital. I'm not going anywhere for the next four weeks. You have all my numbers including hospital, home, and office. Don't hesitate to call."

Bernstein stopped over that night. He didn't find any change from Jessica's description earlier in the day.

Days passed slowly. Anna worsened.

"Bernie, her mouth hurts. There're white patches developing."

"I'll send a prescription for the infection. Follow the directions. Sounds like she has a fungal infection called Monilia. I'll come by this evening to check. Her white blood count is down to one thousand, along with a drop in everything else."

He came by. Anna was in her bedroom with Jessica and Bella. Anna lay back, head resting on the pillows. She remained like that for a few minutes and then started crying. "My mouth burns. Do something."

He gowned up as usual and walked over to the side of her bed, squeezed her hand, and felt for her pulse. "I'm afraid you're dehydrated. It's due to the chemotherapy. We have to get more fluids into you." He looked at Bella. "There's plenty of ice cream in the freezer. Give her as much as you can. Anna, eat it as often as possible. Like every two hours. More often if you like."

She was more comfortable before therapy. Look what I did.

Anna asked, "When will this stop?"

"Not for a week or longer. It depends on how well your body is able to deal with the therapy. You have to eat. Ice cream is good for the sore mouth. It'll give you nutrition."

"A week?" Anna started to cry again.

"It takes that long for the chemo to damage the cancer cells. Sometimes longer, but you will get better. Remember that."

Oncologists are Barbarians. One day they'll look at this treatment and wonder what the hell was wrong with those guys. They weren't doctors. They were sadists.

The next day he was booked solid. Yet his mind kept wandering back to Anna.

I never should have started this.

Stop it, Bernstein. You did the right thing.

Crap. So did Custer.

The intercom interrupted his thoughts with a screech.

"Goddamn machine." He picked it up. "Who's this?"

"Dr. Bernstein, you know perfectly well. It's Maria."

"What now? I thought I fired you."

"I decided to give you another chance."

"Oh. Well, what is it?"

"Better take this call. It's from Marge Whitestone's daughter."

With a sigh, he did as instructed.

"Dr. Bernie, can you come over tonight? Mom wants to speak to you."

"She does? Okay, I'll be over after office hours."

Bernie saw his last patient, made a few phone calls, and drove to the Whitestones' home. As usual, he knocked, didn't wait for an answer, and walked in.

Jo was the first to see him.

"Oh, thank God. Bernie, she's been calling for you all day."

"Has something changed?"

George came in from another room, took Bernie's arm. "I don't know what's going on, doc. Marge is demanding to see you. Last night she kept calling for you in her sleep."

Jo looked at her father and then at Bernstein. "Ma always wants to see you, but this time it's different. Please, Doctor, you're not a magician, but she needs help."

He took off his coat. "I assume she's in the same room."

They nodded, and the three walked into the bedroom.

It was dark, with one light on a night table next to Marge's side. There was water in a glass pitcher and lemon swabs sitting in a container next to a glass. The bed was large enough for two. George's side still held his form, along with disheveled blankets.

She lay on her back. Her skin was pale, her eyelids stuck together, and her mouth dry. Jo found a lemon swab at the bedside and used it to moisten her mother's mouth. Marge opened her eyes, looked everyone over, and focused on Bernstein. "Sonny, sit over here." She motioned the family out of the room.

Once they left, she made sure the door was closed. She grabbed his hands, and tears filled her eyes. "I've been telling you all along that this cancer is my fault. I can't die without telling George the truth. Jo is not his daughter."

Bernstein spoke softly. "Tell me about it."

"When we were first married, we wanted a family very badly. After three years of trying, I couldn't get pregnant. We started fighting every day." She stopped, motioned for some lemon swabs.

Bernie rubbed the swab against her lips and offered her water.

Marge took a sip and continued. "I met a man who was exciting and made me laugh. We had an affair that lasted two months. I knew it was wrong and broke it off." She stopped, looked around the room, and checked the closed door again. Marge started to shiver. "Sonny, there's a blanket in… that closet. Get it for me."

He did as he was told.

Once the blanket was in place, she warmed up and went on with the story. "It took three weeks for me to realize that I was pregnant. It was my beautiful Jo." Bernstein felt a chill.

It took a few minutes for her to gain control. Marge sobbed and then tried to pull herself up in bed to no avail. Bernie realized what she was doing and helped lift her into position.

"I can't die... without telling... It's my sin. I'll go to... hell... if I don't tell... him." Tears ran down her face. Neither spoke. Marge looked at him. "Help me."

Bernstein thought for a moment. "Marge, you know more about farming than most men, but let me ask you a question. Suppose a man comes across a plowed field and throws corn kernels over the field and then walks away and never comes back."

Bernie's mouth was dry. He took one of the lemon swabs and sucked on it and then continued. "Time passes; another man comes by and sees small shoots sprouting. The field is a mess— weeds all over, rocks in the way of plants. There's one corn shoot on top of the next."

Bernie stopped. He took a drink of water from Marge's cup and offered her some. She declined. "Keep going, sonny. I'm listening."

"This second man starts tending the field. He gets rid of the weeds and thins the shoots. He fertilizes, waters, and finally there is a wonderful crop of corn."

There was a moment of silence. Marge turned from her back onto her side, facing Bernie.

"Marge, who's the farmer? The first man who threw the kernels and then left, or the second man who tended the stalks and raised a beautiful crop?"

She didn't say a word. Time passed. Slowly she spoke. "So you think I shouldn't say anything?"

"Yes, I agree with you, but that's up to you. The three of you are a very close family and love each other. George is Jo's father."

She looked at him for a time and then motioned for him to leave. "Get out of here and let me think."

Bernstein left the room, and Jo went in to comfort her mother. In less than three minutes, she ran back out, crying, "Mama isn't breathing." Bernie followed George and Jo back into the room.

Marge Whitestone had died.

The family looked at him. George wanted to know what she had said.

"Marge wanted to make sure that when she died, you both knew how much she loved you."

Arrangements were made, the funeral-home driver arrived, and Bernie signed the necessary papers. "Let me know if there's anything more I can do. You're always welcome to come into the office and talk."

Bernstein slowly opened the door to his Jeep and stuck the key into the ignition. He took a deep breath and drove the car slowly out of the driveway onto the road. The steering wheel was cold, his foot couldn't find the accelerator, and he was in total darkness.

Shit! I forgot to turn on the lights.

He reacted quickly, pulled the light switch, and avoided hitting a tree. The car rolled on into the night.

Chapter 30

Days passed. Anna's blood work was drawn and checked every two days. Bernie stopped by nightly to examine and give her needed fluids.

"Hey, kid, you're pushing twelve days now. Any change?"

"My stomach still hurts, but I passed gas today. I felt better."

"Well, there you go. The longest journey starts with a fart. I bet the smell would make a maggot gag."

Bella interrupted, "Dr. Bernstein, this is no time for jokes. She's sick, and you're joking with her."

"I'm sorry, Bella. You're right, of course. I feel the pressure, and jokes help me."

Bella nodded, accepting his apology. "What was the blood count today? I'm sure you have it."

"That's the good news. Anna's white blood counts are still very low, but they've bottomed out for the last three days. The platelets are starting to come up. I think her blood work is at the low point and should start to improve."

Jessica looked at Bernie and then asked about Anna's mouth. "Her mouth looks worse today. She's not able to swallow anything, not even the ice cream."

"Okay, I'll change the prescription again. Hopefully, this one will work."

He told them he'd bring two IV bags of fluid the next day. "It'll rehydrate her."

He drove home listening to Miles Davis playing "Kind of Blue." The soothing classic piece made him smile.

At noon the next day, Bernie showed up with grilled zucchini caprese sandwiches to share with Toni at her office.

"Oh, you remembered me. What happened? I thought you found another girlfriend."

"Not on your life. I can only handle one shikseh at a time, and you are a major-league handful."

He took the sandwiches. "They're cold." He found a scalpel and clamps and put the works into the autoclave for a minute. "Presto—the greatest sandwich ever made."

"The coffee is ready." She poured a cup for each of them. "Okay, now bring me up to date about Anna."

This he did while munching on his sandwich. "We're in the critical phase of the treatment. Her blood counts are at the bottom but have been steady for the last couple of days. I have a feeling that the tumors are shrinking ever so slightly." He looked at the sandwich. "No, this is yours," he said and took hers from her. "I have the extra onions and garlic." He gave back the one he had started.

Toni shook her head. "You just started treating her a little over a week ago."

"I agree with you. That's why I think I'm nuts, but I do feel a change. It happens."

Toni shook her head. "I hope you're right. Just make sure you give her plenty of fluids over the next few days."

He nodded.

"By the way, Hampton sent his nurse here for Anna's slides. Seems he wanted to send them out for a second opinion."

"You mean Her Royal Stuffiness showed up?"

"Good description. Said her name was Snore or something like that."

"Ah yes, Ms. Boor. What did you tell her?"

"Why, I said that I'd be delighted to give her the slides if Dr. Hampton is a consultant on the case. No, says she, while her nose inspected the ceiling tiles. He is the chief of medicine of this hospital."

Bernie laughed. "Well, kiss my ass."

Toni was on top of the situation. "No, Bernstein, I was calm and ladylike. I said that Dr. Hampton needed a release from Anna's mother."

Bernie made a face. "Bella wouldn't do that in a million years."

"You're right." Toni laughed. "Boor said they didn't have one; he's the chief of medicine. I smiled demurely and then informed her that she couldn't have the slides. This led to a heated discussion. She insisted that Dr. Hampton did not need anyone's consent. Then she stuck out her chest and announced again that he's the chief of medicine and doesn't need anyone's permission. I smiled again. Informed her I'm the chief of pathology, and I won't release anything without a consent form from the family." Toni stopped, took a drink of coffee, and stood up. "Boor became abusive. At that point I told her to get out and tell Hampton to call me." She smiled that lovely smile of hers. "So far he hasn't called, and it won't do him a bit of good if he does."

Bernie took another bite of his sandwich and helped it down with a sip of coffee. "I had another of those strange events occur that I wanted to speak to you about." He then told her of Marge Whitestone's death.

Neither spoke. It seemed time had stopped until Toni broke the silence. "It shows us how little we know about the human body. I've read of mystics who can will themselves to die. In this case, you gave your patient permission."

"It's all part of the art that we practice," he responded.

The two finished their meal, thinking. "Toni, you are the best," Bernie said as he left.

That evening he stopped off at Anna's house with a few bags of fluid.

"How's she doing?"

"Bernie, Anna has a lot of cramps." Jessica had on her nurse's uniform.

She's finally into the program.

Jessica continued, "Her mouth is still full of Monilia patches, and she's not eating a thing. On top of that, Anna's temperature is a little over a hundred."

"Damn it. How's her skin?"

"Dry, and her urine is dark—almost orange."

"The intravenous fluids I gave her didn't do much good. She'll need more. In the morning I'll pick up a bag of plasma and deliver it to you to start a drip. Jessica, you just have to monitor it. I'll be back later in the day with more fluids."

That next evening, Bernstein headed over straight from work. He started a bag of fluid. Anna fell asleep. Bernie, Jessica, and Bella spent the next two hours talking. He shared the good news that her white blood count was now up to a thousand. "She's getting better."

Bernie told Jessica that she'd have to remove the IV, as he had to get home. Anna woke up. "Dr. Bernie, I know I'm going to be all right."

"Of course you'll be fine—back in school in no time. You're going through the worst of the therapy, but you'll be good as new."

"I just want the stomach pain to stop. I haven't gone to the bathroom in a long time."

"Once your bowels open up, you'll feel a lot better. Save your first stool. The Smithsonian would probably like it for display in an odor-proof booth."

Bella gave him a scowl. He apologized.

Anna started to stir about in bed and poked at his facemask.

"You look terrible in a mask." She pouted.

"The nurses seem to think I'm charming and look a bit like Ben Casey." That got him a weak punch. "Okay, I'm not hanging around any longer to be insulted. The lab guy will be here in two days, and I'll be over during the early evening." Before getting into his Jeep, he looked up, saw a shooting star, and made a wish.

When Bernstein drove to the house two days later, a surprise greeted him. Anna was sitting upright in a chair.

"Look at you! I can't believe it."

"Yep, Dr. Bernie, and guess what? I had my first poop today. My stomach feels much better."

"How's your mouth?"

"Better. Look."

He peered in. Anna's mouth was clear. She no longer had Monilia.

"Dr. Bernie, are you crying?"

"No… Nah. Must be my allergies."

The family gathered around, and he told them the rest of the good news. Anna's blood was significantly better. She was out of the woods.

"We can plan on another month's treatment." *Oh my God, another month.* "We'll have to wait two more weeks before treatment. Her body has to recover from the ordeal we just put her through."

They were quiet until Bella spoke. "Bernie, will she have these side effects every time?"

He looked at the floor and then at Anna. "Hopefully not as severe. I'm afraid the dose has to be much the same each month."

Anna started to cry. Jessica held her close to her chest. "I know, pumpkin, but you're getting so much better."

Bernstein looked at Bella and then Anna. He nodded in agreement. "Anna, basically we're feeling our way. Honestly, I don't know how long, but at least you're getting better."

Anna stopped crying. She held out her small hand to Bernie and gave a squeeze. Her smile lit up the room.

He drove home that night with the windows wide open.

What's that smell? Spring!

He pulled over to the side of the road and listened to the waves lapping against the shore.

Anna dodged the first bullet. Now what? Repeat the chemotherapy. Lower the dose? It would avoid side effects. Might not work. Same dose? Might just kill her. Take one month at a time. It's going to work!

Bernie stared into the night sky. The North Star was clearly visible. "I have direction now. Anna will have to get slightly lower doses."

Chapter 31

The next few months passed with the same problems. Anna on the brink of a crisis, the family full of fear, and Bernstein—well, Bernstein was Bernstein.

It's going to work. She's getting better. The tumors are smaller. Damn, she can't have come this far and not make it.

And Anna came through the worst. He, on the other hand, continued house calls, making minor adjustments to the chemotherapy. The doses had their effect. Four months after therapy began, Anna was alive. She had no hair on her head, mouth sores every two weeks, and diarrhea. The masses decreased each month.

In the fifth month, they could no longer be felt.

Now what?

"How long should I continue the treatment?" Bernie said to no one during his morning run. "She'll need one more month. If all goes well, I'll stop... maybe."

He continued to treat Anna at home for the next month. One summer day he stopped over at the house with a basket of goodies.

Tomatoes, I love tomatoes, especially from my garden, and this year I have piles of beautiful Big Boys and cherry tomatoes—even cukes, potatoes, and one eggplant. I've never been able to grow a stupid eggplant. So far, a great summer. Everything has grown.

Bernstein got out with his basket. Anna was playing catch in the front yard with Earl.

"Anna, stop running so fast. You'll get hurt," Bernie called out.

"Hey, farmer Bernie, catch," she said, and a Nerf ball bounced off his head.

"Easy, kid, I'm carrying goodies from my garden."

"Oh yummy, you grew Twinkies."

"Nah, the Twinkie seeds didn't take. Here's second best. They're called vegetables. I was offered big bucks for this stuff."

That got him a face from Anna and a soft mouthing from Earl.

"Can't this rotten dog accept me by now? He did when you were sick. It's been months now. I think he's a slow learner."

"He likes you."

"Really? Supposed he didn't?"

"He'd sit on the porch and sulk."

"Wow, can I get him to hate me?"

She laughed, and the three walked into the house where Jessica and Bella greeted them.

"Jessica, what's Anna's weight?"

"Ninety-five this morning."

Unbelievable! She's supposed to be dead. He shook his head. "Wow."

He examined Anna. She was normal, and so was the blood work.

Maybe it's time to stop the chemotherapy?

Anna asked if she could go back to school. "It starts this week."

Bernie shook his head. "No, Anna needs one more month of therapy. Then we can talk about school."

Get Anna through each week. Worry about next week. Keep her alive. I never thought about school. Gotta think.

"School? I thought you graduated."

"You know I didn't finish the seventh grade."

"What? You can't be; you're in college."

"I'm eleven," she asserted, standing with her hands on her hips.

"That's impossible. I don't take care of kids. There must be a mistake." He couldn't contain his laugh. That got him a punch.

"Bella, I don't know. I'll have to get advice on this one. My gut feeling is to give an additional month. Her tumors have disappeared as far as I can measure. I'd like to give one more treatment. Anna is prone to infections as long as treatments are continuing. Get a home teacher for this semester."

That seemed to satisfy everyone other than Anna. Bernie didn't feel much better about the decision.

I'm hanging on. It's time to let go. I'm not letting go?

Bernstein called his old professor. "Bernie, give it another month. Then call me."

Six weeks passed and he called again. "Hey, Dave. Anna is normal. I can't find evidence of Hodgkin's. So what do you think I should do?"

"Stop the treatment. She's been free of disease for three months. It's time to give it a rest."

"I'm afraid... I know you're right. Treatment can't go on forever, but I'm afraid to let go. I'm even treating her at home for luck. Can you imagine? I'm afraid to change a thing."

"Bernie, stop it. It's the chemotherapy. What is it? Do you think you haven't helped the girl?"

"I don't know. I picked the right set of drugs. But why?"

"You have to understand that oncologists are scientists and mystics. At times it seems like magic. It's not. You entered an area that's not understood, and you succeeded. For Christ's sake, accept it."

"Dave, this is ironic. Anna is a rarity, and she's driving me nuts."

"Finally, you're beginning to understand something that I've been trying to teach you for years."

Bernie could hear Schaffer swallowing a drink—most likely a vodka martini without the vermouth, his favorite at this hour.

Dave went on. "The chemo won't stop a relapse. Besides, if you keep on with the drugs, it's more likely she'll die from them."

Bernie nodded. "I know, but do you think she's cured?"

"Of course not. The other shoe will drop, but that doesn't change anything. You did great. Accept it."

"Thanks, Dave." They hung up.

He's right. Sit back. Wait.

Bernstein sat back in his chair, took some deep breaths, and hoped someone above was watching.

He stopped treatment and watched her. In late fall, Anna went back to school, first three days a week, then full time.

His lunchtime meetings with Toni continued. They were both becoming innovative regarding meals. The winner was usually Middle Eastern. One day, he showed up with grilled Kasseri cheese in a pita pocket containing hummus and cucumber thinly sliced along with a fattoush salad.

Toni remarked that it was her favorite and bit into the sandwich. While chewing, she asked how Anna was doing off the therapy.

"She's fine, but, Toni, I still don't understand what happened. I found chemotherapy protocols similar to the one I used if not the same. Some worked, others didn't."

"Bernstein, why are you so popular with your patients?"

He shrugged. "I'm like a shaman. Everyone is scared shitless of a diagnosis of cancer. I'm the one that can make them better for a short time."

Toni smiled. "No, dummy. You're so damn shortsighted. Bernie, you're good because you have a human touch. It's essential in the healing process."

Bernie felt heat rise in his face. "I will grant you that we have the ability to overcome more than we think. And yes, a positive attitude is essential. I don't think I'm better than everyone else, but I've come to agree with you. We need control of our bodies along with our minds."

They spent the rest of lunch eating and telling stories.

Chapter 32

It was another long, tense day for Bernie. As he ascended the stairs from the foyer, he heard Russell's unmistakable shrill voice screaming, "You two-timing bastard, get out of my house."

He stepped into the living room and found Russell, all five feet and four inches of him, standing with his nose to Rob's chest.

Leah was sitting on a comfortable living-room chair, while the four boys stationed themselves about the fireplace, taking in the scene.

"Russell, please, you have to stop this yelling. I've apologized a hundred times. I've written to you, and you ignore my letters. I miss you." With that, he reached for Russell.

"You take your dirty hands off me. Rob, you're nothing but a… a manizer! A regular trollop."

Bernie got involved. "Russell, a trollop is a woman."

"Well, Rob is a man version. On top of that, he's a whore… a gigolo. Now, you just get out of my house this very minute."

Rob started crying. "Please, Russell. It'll never happen again. I promise. I have to have you home with me."

Russell walked about the room while Rob watched. Leah stood up and walked over. "You have to stop doing this to Russell. I know how hurt he's been. You're making his heart condition worse."

Bernie looked at his wife. *Heart condition? What heart condition?*

Rob hugged Russell. "I didn't know you had a heart problem. Russell, don't worry. I promise to take care of you for the rest of your life."

Bernie was confused. *Funny; I didn't know of the heart condition.*

Leah glared at Rob. "That's a bad turn of words. You mean you'll care for him forever," she said with a wink at Bernie.

She's throwing around Jewish guilt.

Russell put his hand on his chest gently. "I'll think about it. This isn't the first time you've gone off, but it'll be the last. From now on, consider yourself on a trial basis."

With that, both men hugged. Rob tried to kiss Russell, but he turned away. "Rob, you must wait. I'm not ready yet. Besides, the boys are here."

"Let's go out to dinner. It's on me," Rob announced. Russell allowed his partner to hold his hand as they all walked out the door. The packing would start in the morning.

Chapter 33

Bernie gave up crossed fingers and knocks on wood and had Anna come to the office for checkups. The chemotherapy stopped. She looked great, and the exams stayed normal. Just to be safe, he insisted that she wear her hospital gown and bring Earl to the office.

"No reason to take chances," he announced.

While making hospital rounds one day, he heard a commotion on Jessica's floor.

Jessica was pleading, "Dr. DeJesus, watch your language."

"I don't care. Those stupid sons of bitches at the university think no one knows anything. Look at this shit."

Bernstein arrived on the floor to see Jessica reading an article in a major medical journal that Carlos DeJesus had shoved in her face. He, on the other hand, was standing atop her desk.

She became pale, slumped into a chair, and started to cry.

DeJesus thrust the magazine at Bernstein. "Do you see the crap they publish? Have you read this article? It's the latest edition."

"No, Carlos, I've been too busy dealing with wacko doctors yelling at nothing."

Bernie scanned the article. The title read, "Unusual Case of Lymphoma Misdiagnosed as Hodgkin's Disease." Initials were used to describe the patient; they were Anna's. There was no question that this was a teaching exercise about Bernie's patient.

The case study made it clear that while the diagnosis was difficult, the young girl did not have Hodgkin's disease. It was a lymphoma, and not any lymphoma but one that did not respond to therapy.

The summary stated that she had been sent back to her family doctor for terminal care. The last line read, "I'm sure she's died by now."

Bernstein reread the article while Jessica cried and DeJesus had his tantrum.

Bernstein looked at DeJesus. "Carlos, you're the epitome of tact."

He then walked over to Jessica, put his arm around her, and said, "This won't happen. Anna is fine."

Jessica cried, "I can't believe that they feel she died. My precious Anna is alive. She's alive…" and she held onto Bernie tightly.

Months passed. All good. Anna no longer suffered the delayed effects of treatment. Her strength started coming back, and she gained weight.

He stopped by one evening on the way home and commented on how well she looked.

"Yep. I'm graduating from the eighth grade next month. It's been a year and a half since I went back to school. I feel wonderful."

Christ! Almost two years free of disease. She might be cured. What the hell happened? Is she cured? I don't know.

Four years came and went. Nothing happened. Bernstein still felt uneasy and provided no more than vague reassurances to the family.

He developed regular contacts with many of the professors in Boston. "Bernie, stop worrying so much. Anna is going to be fine. She's years past the two-year mark for Hodgkin's. That usually means a cure. You sound like a Jewish grandmother."

"I know, but this is such a strange disease, I don't think it follows the usual pattern."

"You're right, but there's nothing to do about it. Just watch her."

Anna started coming into the office every four months, still wearing the original hospital gown.

It was in the fifth year that he received a frantic phone call from Bella. "Bernie, Anna awoke this morning with a swollen face. She was fine yesterday."

"Any fever? Or pain?"

"No fever, but it hurts."

He breathed a sigh of relief. "Not to worry. Bring her right in."

They both came in within the hour. Indeed, the left side of her face was swollen and tender but not the lymph nodes.

Bernstein examined her. "Your mouth is very dry. Haven't you been drinking fluids?"

"Not really. My mouth is usually dry, although not this bad."

"What did you do yesterday?"

"Nothing—just school, came home, and went to sleep."

"Sleep? Why were you so tired?"

She made a face. "The crazy gym teacher had us running a mile and then doing calisthenics. It's been going on for days. Am I okay? Graduation is in a week."

"Well, in that case we'll have to be very aggressive. One week, you say. Hmm. Yep, do the sour ball treatment."

They both looked at him. Bernstein laughed.

"Sorry for teasing, but all that chemotherapy and radiation closed your salivary gland ducts. You have a backup of saliva. Sour balls will open up the ducts, and you'll be fine."

There was a collective sigh of relief. Bella asked, "Bernie, is Anna cured? You keep evading the answer. It's not like you."

He shrugged. "Most likely. Hodgkin's acts strangely. Very few cancers have a two-year period after which patients free of the disease can be considered cured. Hodgkin's is one of those diseases that two years free means cured."

He saw confusion on their faces and re-explained. "In other words, if someone with Hodgkin's lives for two years without a flare-up, it's assumed they're cured. But the studies are all based on first-time treatments. Anna has been treated more than twice."

Bella and Anna wanted more assurances.

"I'm afraid there aren't any other than what I've told you. I guess she's cured, but I don't know."

Anna sucked on the sour balls; the swelling went away. She graduated high school five and a half years after being given up for dead.

Chapter 34

"Dr. Bernstein, Dr. Powers is on the phone from Boston."

"Maria, I was meditating. What the hell did I tell you?"

"But Doctor, he's calling from the university."

He gave up and answered the phone with a cheery, "Hi, Al."

"Bernie, I'm calling about Manuel Braz, the fellow you sent up last week. I saw him the same day and had the pathologist look at the slides. He agrees that it's an aggressive lymphoma. It seems they give a lot more attention to anything you send up." Bernie felt his face redden. "By the way, I heard that Anna's doing very well. How long has it been? Must be eight years now."

"Yep, she'll be graduating college next year. I'm following her every six months. She's normal other than missed menstrual periods. I'm sure her ovaries were wiped out from the chemotherapy and radiation."

"A small price to pay, by my guess." Powers coughed into the phone to end the comment. He went on. "I've been waiting for you to submit the case study to one of the medical journals. So where is it?"

"Nowhere. I still have no idea what worked. The same drugs have been used since on other cases of lymphoma and Hodgkin's. At times they're successful and other times not. In Anna's case it worked, but I have no idea why." Bernie stopped, scratched his nose. "Al, I can't feel the sense that I did anything… If only I knew why it worked."

"That's ridiculous, Bernie. Most oncologists are humbled treating cancer patients. You have to get used to the fact that there are reasons that are just not explainable but will be in the future. Meanwhile, you did a great job and had a lot of guts. You should be proud of yourself."

"Maybe…"

They chatted some more, and Bernstein said one day he'd write about it, but not in a medical journal. "Maybe in the *Journal of Unnatural Phenomena.*"

They laughed and said good-byes.

Afterword

Twenty years passed. Bernie had semiretired and had seen Anna only infrequently over the previous few years. She was a woman of thirty-one when she called him.

"Dr. Bernie, I want you to meet someone. Can you stop by the house today?"

"For you, I'd do anything. Be there at six."

He drove up to the house. Anna was playing ball with a small boy. Jessica and Bella were watching from the porch.

"Hi, kid. A new addition?"

"Single-parent adoption. He understands Ukrainian. We flew over a month ago after setting up the adoption. I told them I was healthy. They had a doctor check me over."

Bernstein smiled. "Of course you're healthy." He gave her a hug and scratched the boy on the head.

It's an improvement over Earl; at least this little guy didn't bite me.

Bernstein had a cup of coffee with Jessica and Bella. They watched Anna and the boy play. When he rose to leave, Anna came over and pointed to the boy. "His name is Bernie."

Thirty years after Bernstein first saw Anna, his precious Leah died of a so-called curable lymphoma. He received sympathy cards from many, including Bella, Jessica, Anna, and young Bernie.

Some live. Some die.

Go figure.